One Night At The 4/26

Kevin Densmore

Published by Kevin Densmore, 2022.

This is a work of fiction. Similarities to real people, places, or events are entirely coincidental.

ONE NIGHT AT THE 4/26

First edition. April 26, 2022.

ISBN: 979-8201162108

Written by Kevin Densmore.

Also by Kevin Densmore

Scary Things Happen in Lakewood
Scary Things Happen in Lakewood
Scary Things Happen in Lakewood 2
Scary Things Happen in Lakewood 3

Stories to Inspire and Tales that Terrify
Stories to Inspire and Tales That Terrify.
Stories to Inspire and Tales that Terrify (Volume Two)
Stories to Inspire and Tales That Terrify.(Volume Three)

Standalone
Strange 80's State of Mind
Savage 90's State Of Mind
The Devil's Missing Children
What the Rain Washes Away
Sweet 70's State of Mind
Pesky Little Sleeve Hearts
One Night At The 4/26

Table of Contents

For Brandon....................1
Introduction: Let's talk about my favorite hole in the wall....................3
Prologue: (1962 through 1975) – What was left upstairs....................7
Chapter 1: (2022) - Welcome to The 4/26....................17
Chapter 2: (2022) - Meet The Players....................23
Chapter 3: 2022 - Round One Begins....................33
Chapter 4: (1975 through 1979) - The Child Grows....................39
Chapter 5: 2022 - A Fatal Low Ton....................45
Chapter 6: 2022 - What's in the Basement?....................55
Chapter 7: 2022 - A Tempest Has Arrived....................61
Chapter 8: 1980-1984 - Lessons in Beer and Fear....................69
Chapter 9: 2022 - Division Begins....................79
Chapter 10: 2022 - Something on the Dance Floor....................87
Chapter 11: 2022 - A Bloody Hat Trick....................91
Chapter 12: 1985-1991 - Spores and the Mess They Make....................99
Chapter 13: 2022 - Basement Tragedy....................109
Chapter 14: 2022- Nightmare Upstairs....................117
Chapter 15: -2022- A Llama's Bad Advice....................123
Chapter 16: 1992-2000 - A Young Man's Malice....................131
Chapter 17: 2022 - Fighting Back Up....................143
Chapter 18: 2022 - Straight In and Straight Out....................149
Chapter 19: 202 2- A Second Deadly Rumble....................155
Chapter 20: 2001-2022 - Everything Under His Control....................163
Chapter 21: 2022 - The Final Fight....................177
Chapter 22: 2022 - Three In A Bed....................183
Chapter 23: 2022 - Help Arrives....................191
Epilogue: 2022-2023 - A Hard Year....................197
Author's Notes: Fun Facts Are Fun....................201

This Book is Dedicated to my Mother Anita, I did it Mom!!!!

And to Brandon Land Rest easy good sir.

Edited By: Becka Anderson

Special Gore Consultant: Jenn Mitchell

Cover Photography, Lettering, and addtional artwork: Jenn 'Sunshine" Mitchell

Cover Models: Cris Breck & Christian Flores

For Brandon

As I began writing this book, a man I had never met had passed away. His name is Brandon Land. Even though I never met him beyond knowing about his passing, several people at the bar knew this man well and loved him. He was like a family member to most. He was kind, selfless, and a friend to all. Since his passing, I have heard many heartwarming stories about the man he was. I dedicate this book to his memory as a favor to everyone who knew him and lent their names to this story. I genuinely wish I had the pleasure to have gotten to know him. Not knowing him does not mean I cannot do him and his loved ones a favor by this one simple act of dedicating this book to him. Rest easy good sir. I am sure we would have been friends.

Introduction: Let's talk about my favorite hole in the wall

I have never been much of a barfly; actually, I am not much of a drinker. But yet, I wound up finding a friendly home away from home all the same.

This book was inspired because a friend of mine begged people via a social media platform to come and join her for a night of playing darts. Being the naive, bored, former semi-okay dart player of years long gone, I decided, "Hey, why not?" I thought it was only going to be one night. It quickly evolved into me joining a dart league where my team, which was never the same from week to week, was quickly demolished. My team quickly moved to last place. Understandably, someone had to come in last place. The fact that I never had a cohesive team truly bothered me. So I did the only thing someone in my situation might do.

I quit.

Now don't get me wrong, I liked the place. It was a nice little hole in the wall bar (and I say this with love). Everyone I met was fantastic, and this made for some great acquaintances. I was never in it for the long haul. Then something happened. I, the self-proclaimed "King Antisocial," made friends. I started to like these people.

And, apparently, they started to like me.

At first, I thought it was an act of desperation, that they just needed another body to fill the dart league's roster. But it turned out to be more than that. These players, the regulars, considered me a friend. Soon I found camaraderie among what I figured would be a permanent group of strangers, and well, I became enamored. Quite honestly, I fell in love with the place. So when they asked me to please return and promised me a team, I said, "Ok." I was still skeptical. But, what else was I going to do on a Tuesday night?

So, I continued to play darts. This decision, of course, led to interactions away from the bar. My good friend and the bar's owner said I could probably write a book on the bar with all the stuff that happens. A brief joking exchange on social media led to this book. Somehow that interaction caused a lightbulb to go off in my head. After a moment of recall, a story started to form.

You see, during my fourth week there (my mind is a trap, so yes, I know it was the fourth week), a horrible storm raged through my small town. That was when I noticed just how bad of a shape the bar was. Now I must note that the bar resides on the first floor of a two-story building (with gutted apartments on the second floor), yet, as the rain came down, rivers of water somehow flowed through the ceiling into the bar area. It should not be the case, but it was. I watched as regulars and bartenders ran and fetched buckets and garbage cans to catch the rain, and I felt a newfound faith in humanity. I also felt pity for the owner and rage towards the landlord. But it was also not my business. So I stayed out of it.

Weeks later, after befriending and getting to know everyone, I honestly wanted to help. I felt there was nothing I could do except support the place. Then this book happened.

Soon after that social media interaction and during my first week with my new team and new dart season, I was allowed in the upstairs apartments. After witnessing the horrible conditions above the bar, I started to form this story. That vision suddenly became a lesson in chaos, a warning about slumlords, a fucking gonzo violent exploration of human emotions and mold. It became a horror show.

I won't spoil anything, but I will say that an actual person inspires nearly every character in this book; they even allowed me to use their names. Two of those individuals are on the cover, while another one of them edited this lesson in mayhem.

I am completely honored that April, the owner of Pub 4-26, allowed me to use her bar as a backdrop for this story. Yes, as a writer, I did take a lot of liberties, but our interactions while playing darts remain the same.

So if you are ever in Plano, Illinois, especially on a Tuesday night, come on down to good 'ole Pub 4-26. I will probably be there laughing with my new group of friends. If I'm not, I am home writing another tale. But, have a drink, and maybe later I can take you into the vacant apartments above... Because, after all, that's where the real horror lies.

Prologue: (1962 through 1975) – What was left upstairs

When Zayan immigrated from India to the United States in April of 1962, he had only one thing on his mind, to pursue the American dream. He had saved up all his financial earnings as a street vendor to escape his overcrowded country. He had a vision for success; the postcards he often received from his cousin, Amir, inspired him. He realized that while attempting to rise out of poverty in India could be quite a chore, with the right work ethic, achieving success in America was manageable and relatively easy if you knew where to look.

The hard part was saving up his money and leaving his entire family behind. However, at the ripe age of nineteen, Zayan had managed to save a total of twenty-seven million rupees (which was roughly over 350,000 American dollars). He booked a flight to Chicago, Illinois. That was indeed the challenging part because as he said goodbye to his family, Zayan was immediately told never to return, mainly because they considered him a disgrace to the family. Zayan still departed for Chicago. His cousin, Amir, met Zayan at the airport. The moment he walked out of the terminal is where he started his pursuit of success and fortune.

Amir had told Zayan that the first thing he needed to do was apply for his citizenship, which he did after staying in America for only a week. He began to look for his next pot of gold in the melting pot that was Chicago. Six months, a few tough questions, and eight hundred dollars later, Zayan was a proud American citizen.

Amir suggested that Zayan invest in a restaurant venture, and together, the two started an Indian Cuisine restaurant that also delivered. They cut corners on the menu to keep overhead low, but apparently that did not matter. Their restaurant was different. The Chicago residents could not get enough of their food, lining Amir and Zayan's pockets and swelling their bank accounts.

The restaurant industry was Amir's dream; while Zayan was happy with his wealth, he wanted something more. Zayan noticed that the landlord who owned their restaurant's building made nearly as much as them just off rent. Their restaurant, located in only one of their landlord's ten buildings, made the situation even more compelling. Zayan then realized what he wanted to do. For lack of a better term, he wanted to be a high-profile landlord.

Zayan began to look for vacant buildings and found Chicago was either hit or miss. Many buildings he looked out were too run down to turn a profit, while others were way out of his price range. During the summer of 1965, while he was searching for a building, Zayan met his future wife, Sheila.

Sheila was a waitress at one of the restaurants Zayan was interested in buying. The landlord had decided to stop paying the bank. One day, without any notification, that landlord cleaned out his bank accounts and left the country. (This quick departure was standard when people sought loans from the Chicago mafia representatives. Zayan quickly learned to stay far away from them.) The bank had seized the property and was ready to sell it to the highest bidder, starting at a low price that Zayan found very reasonable; it was practically a steal if he was being honest. As Zayan was inspecting the place, he was shocked to see that the bank had allowed the restaurant to stay open, but with a closing sign in the window, he knew that the restaurant would not remain in operation for long. Zayan took a seat in the booth at the far end of the restaurant and stared out the window when Sheila sauntered over to take his order.

"What will it be, sugar?" asked the most angelic voice he had ever heard. Zayan turned his head. His eyes locked with Sheila's, and he knew he would spend the rest of his life with her.

He did not speak, but the way her brown eyes locked with his, he knew she felt something, too. "Your name." was all he said, answering her question.

Sheila smiled. At that very moment, he knew he had given her the right answer.

Zayan chose not to purchase the restaurant. After her shift, he did leave with Sheila, which ultimately led them to a beautiful two-year courtship.

Sheila convinced Zayan to look for properties outside of Chicago during their courtship. He purchased several buildings in outlying communities. His first purchase was a retail space in Plainfield, just two hours from Chicago. Next came a corner lot that he acquired for next to nothing in Yorkville's up-and-coming town. Then twenty minutes south of Yorkville, he discovered the blossoming town of Plano, Illinois. Plano was peaceful and quaint. He found himself practically falling in love. As he made his way down Main Street, he saw a single two-story building with a large sign hanging off the side that read Ruby's Bar and Grille. While that sign was intriguing, it was the one in the window that interested him more.

Taped to the window was a crudely written sign on crisp white paper that said: "For Sale." Underneath was a phone number and where to inquire, and inquire he did. He discovered that the bar and grille sat over a vast basement area that housed the boiler room. There was also a makeshift dance floor that the original owner had installed. The dance floor was a fine selling point Zayan could elevate to entice an aspiring bar and grill owner to rent this location. The bar was fully functional, and the original owner left everything behind. It appeared that finding a renter was going to be a cakewalk. He excitedly purchased that two-story building three days later.

Zayan and Sheila's love flourished. They married, celebrating with a very extravagant wedding during the early months of 1968. Two weeks later, they moved, making Plano their new home.

A few years later, a new bar owner rented the downstairs area of this two-story building in Plano. The bar was named The Lucky Tap. While the bar was great, and the bar owner always paid the rent on time, Zayan had plans for the upstairs portion of the building. Zayan turned the spacious upstairs area into four three-room apartments with as little work as possible and some inexpensive materials. They each had a living/ sleeping area, a kitchen, and a complete bathroom. Perfect for a single person or couple just starting their lives.

The apartments proved to be a success, but the news he received as he moved in the first tenant in the fall of 1971 really excited him. Sheila was with child. After learning that he would become a father, he celebrated by buying the vacant buildings next to the bar. Before his child was born, Zayan owned most of Main Street in this quaint town of Plano, Illinois.

Although Zayan was a fair landlord, he was what most people would call cheap. For example, the upstairs tenants were often angry with their appliances. Although he promised furnished apartments, he always managed to find the devices on clearance or in some second-hand shop. More often than not, the appliances never matched throughout the individual apartments. He had even managed to build a large shed in his backyard where he kept all the appliances that he would rotate out between the four apartments. Zayan would, of course, repair whatever needed attention, but usually in the most cost-efficient way imaginable. This money-pinching led to some constant upkeep. Zayan found the temporary and sometimes questionable fixes got him by, even if his tenants were not too happy with the outcome. These questionable fixes led to the bar closing down on several occasions. Before his son was born, the bar had changed names twice and owners three times.

Zayan had managed to keep all his other buildings going as well, but tenants never seemed to stay past their lease, which led to a lot of different stores gracing his side of Main Street in what would become historic downtown Plano. But Zayan did not care. He relied upon the next someone with a dream, a plan, accompanied with some quick disposable income, that would love a chance to have a shop on Main Street.

On the night of his child's birth came a storm that would nearly bankrupt him. The storm was a raging tempest outside while he was in the hospital with Sheila as she gave birth. Zayan was excited to watch the birth of his child. As he watched his son rip through his wife's womb, he smiled until he saw his son's face. The baby's left eye hung a good two inches lower than the right, giving the impression that the baby's left cheek was melting. The nose was small and nearly non-existent, but the baby's nostrils were huge, leaving the impression that the baby had the nasal cavity of a snake. Under the nose were two perfectly formed lips, but that was the only good thing about the child. As Zayan examined the rest of his child, he saw that the baby's hands did not resemble the hands of a normal baby but had two digits, a thumb, and a rather large pointer finger, giving the illusion that the child had claws. The feet were even worse. With only three extending digits, they looked like something that belonged to a lizard. Each toe was quite long, and they curled on each other as if they were trying to grasp hold of something. The doctor held Zayan's son (who Zayan could tell was a boy even though the baby's penis was misshapen and quite large). And with a fearful look, went to hand the baby to Zayan.

"I'm sorry," the doctor said. Zayan refused to hold his son and turned to leave the hospital room. "Ma'am, would you like to see your son?" the doctor asked Sheila with a slighter stutter in his voice. Zayan was opening the door to the hospital room when he heard his wife begin to scream out, "No!" over and over.

As soon as Zayan was able, he ventured to assess the damage in Plano while Sheila and the baby stayed at the hospital. When Zayan saw the aftermath of what the storm left behind, he almost gave up. Only one of his buildings was left unscathed; this storefront that was, as of right now, a hair salon, laid at the end of his row of buildings. While still standing, the other three suffered severe cosmetic damage to the front, and every window was gone. Unfortunately, it was the second-story building that suffered the most destruction.

Half the roof was gone and was lying crumpled in various places on the street. The swinging sign that had seen several name changes was gone, although later found about a mile away next to the train tracks that ran through Plano. The awnings that hung over the two entrances were also gone; only the holes where it was attached remained. He walked and surveyed the damage done to his buildings. Still, he wasn't really paying attention. Not only did the gods above cause a storm that threatened to destroy his livelihood, but they also thought it would be nice to have his wife give birth to a deformed monster that he was now going to call his son.

The only reason Zayan was on Main Street was to get away from the creature his wife had birthed in the early hours that morning. The state of his buildings was honestly the farthest thing from his mind. Sure, if he put his head down, he could quickly repair the damage done to his buildings. He could probably do so cheaply if he did most of the work himself and bought supplies wholesale. The real problem was the second-story building. The storm only ruined the apartments above it. The bar below was pretty much untouched. The only damage was some broken windows, and the collapsed outside seating area in the back. Yes, his buildings were salvageable. If he threw himself into his project, he would never have to see that hideous beast his wife brought into the world.

Zayan was shocked to see Sheila breastfeeding the baby upon returning to the hospital. He locked eyes with Sheila, walked over, and kissed her forehead. "You know, we can consider adoption," he implored. "And we can try again." "No," Sheila growled. "We were chosen to take care of this creature, so we will! But I will never go through the horrors of childbirth again." She paused and quietly muttered in a sad, disappointing tone, "just to have something like this." Slowly she pushed the blanket covering her son's deformed face, and she stared down at him. "But right now, I think it's best if we tell everyone he died at birth." Zayan nodded his approval and pulled the blanket back over his son's head.

For the next two years, Zayan stayed busy. He managed to repair the single-story damaged storefronts in less than a couple of months. Once he finished the repairs, Zayan moved various businesses into the single-story storefronts. Zayan had another plan for the upstairs apartments of the two-story building. Because he was concocting a plan to hide something away in the apartments above the bar, Zayan was determined to keep rent down and the spirits of his tenants high. He did not want anyone to become suspicious or even angry at him if they did discover what he was hiding. He focused first on the roof. After repairing it, he began to knock down most of the walls in the upstairs apartments. With heavy sound-absorbing carpeting, he padded the floors, which separated the apartments from the downstairs bar area.

While Zayan was steadily at work renovating, Sheila had started to sleep more and more during the day as her depression overtook her. Zayan knew that it was all that disgusting child's fault. He wanted his happiness back, and short of killing the child, he could only think of placing the child in a home> Every attempt was denied as no one wanted the burden of that beast. Zayan finally knew what he would turn the space above the bar into. That was when he turned the apartments into his child's soon-to-be home. The hard part would be finding someone who wanted to become the caretaker of his hideous child. In the meantime, he, and a crew of roughly fifty non-English speaking day laborers, managed to turn the four apartments into one decently sized living space. After two years and several hundred thousand dollars, he completed the repairs, and everything was in place. It was now time for Zayan to put an ad in the paper for a caretaker.

While waiting for someone to answer his ad, he needed to rent the bar area. Zayan had a lot of people showing interest in the bar, but no one had requested to rent it. Soon, a young man with a sizable inheritance took notice of the vacant bar space. Zayan was excited to rent this bar, which would now be known as Friendly's Tap, to a young man named David. Zayan suggested that David reopen the downstairs dance floor and consider having live entertainment. Zayan's literal encouragement was to make as much noise as possible.

Friendly's Tap opened in the summer of 1975. One night after the bar closed, Zayan went into the apartment upstairs carrying his child, who was now three. The child's deformed feet had prevented him from walking. Zayan found himself cursing under his breath as he climbed the stairs with the child in his arms. Zayan had turned the upstairs into essentially a giant day care. It had a fully functional bathroom equipped to handle someone with disabilities. There was an entertainment area with a television and a record player. There were also two bedrooms, one that was more vibrant and colorful than any child could love, while the other was the perfect room for a single adult. The child was asleep, so Zayan walked over to the child's bedroom and gently laid his deformed son on the bed. Zayan then paced the room, waiting for the guest he knew would be arriving soon. Five minutes into his pacing, there was a knock on the downstairs door. Zayan hurried down the stairs and opened the door wide. He found himself staring into the eyes of his newest employee, Patricia. "You're late," He grumbled.

"Yes, but I am here," answered Patricia rather smartly. Zayan was about to say something, but he figured that he needed Patricia more than she needed him right now. Patricia was a fifty-year-old introvert.

When she met the child, she did not seem phased. She had no problem hiding herself and the child away from the world in the apartment he had built above the bar. The caretaker smiled warmly at the child. Zayan questioned if she would be able to perform the duties of this unlikely and seemingly undesirable position. Patricia confirmed that it would be no problem as long as Zayan kept his end of the agreement: keeping her clothed, fed, entertained, and sheltered.

"Where is the child?" asked Patricia as she followed Zayan upstairs. "Sleeping in his room," Zayan quietly responded. Patricia coldly replied, "And my first allowance?" Zayan turned and handed her an envelope that contained four crisp new hundred-dollar bills. "Be certain to never leave the child alone when it is awake." Patricia sighed and then became a bit cross. "I know, and quit calling the child it, okay? Just why is saying "he" that hard? Or better yet, call him by his name!" Zayan turned to say something to Patricia, but before he could speak, she could tell by the shame in the man's eyes what he was about to say.

Shaking her head, "You never named him," she stated with a combination of disappointment and disbelief. "You rich assholes are all the same. Fine! I will name him." Zayan began to say something more but lowered his head. Patricia pushed past him, "You can go. I will take care of this child, but I expect you here once a week to provide me with what I require. I will have a list ready, and maybe you could say hi to your child. But you are probably fine just the way things are. I am warning you, if you fail to show up, I will let the world know what you are hiding here." Zayan shook his head up and down, letting her know he understood. He took his leave, hurrying down the stairs and shutting the door quietly behind him. He felt a weight come off his shoulders and could not wait to get home and tell Sheila they were now finally free.

Patricia walked around the apartment and smiled; she was excited that she would never have to go outside for much ever again. Plus, she had a child she could love. Slowly and quietly, Patricia walked into the child's room and stared down at him. She smiled and said, "Your name is Zeus. You may not be much to the rest of the world, but to me, you will be my world." She slowly brushed the child's hair away from his deformed eye and kissed him on the forehead. Suddenly for the first time in his three years on this Earth, the child had a name, a safe place, and someone that loved him.

Chapter 1: (2022) - Welcome to The 4/26

It was Tuesday when April pulled her Mustang into the first parking spot located in front of the door of her newly acquired bar. Well, it was not freshly acquired as she had owned the place for about three months now. However, the renovated signs with the new name of The 4/26 stood out brightly as they replaced the tired, old, and tattered Friendly's Tap sign.

The original owner of Friendly's Tap had died about four years ago. Unfortunately, when his sons took over, they did not put much time or care into the business or even the actual bar. It appeared that they let the place run into the ground. Mainly because the bar had a certain stigmata surrounding suicides and death. No one really blamed the bar for the horrible things happening around it, but the sons just wanted to be done with it and put little to no effort into it.The site was in such disarray that the landlord, an elderly gentleman, Zayan, who migrated from India, had no choice but to evict them. As soon as April heard that the location was available to rent, she quickly jumped at the chance to finally achieve her long-held dream of owning a bar.

April had been in Friendly's Tap quite a bit in her younger partying years. She knew the bar in and out like the back of her hand. For years Friendly's Tap had acquired the reputation of being just a drink and go kind of bar,and the original owners enjoyed that vibe. The bar and grill area was relatively huge. It consisted of two large main sections separated by a half wall partition. These sections showcased a simple place to eat, drink, and socialize but offered only tables and chairs. There were no other entertainment options at the moment. April desired her bar to be more than a local watering hole. So when

Zayan presented an offer that appeared damn near too good to be true, April jumped at the chance to own the place. As with everything in life, when something seems too good to be true, there is always a catch. Zayan emphasized that she must agree to two stipulations:

One: April would be responsible for all upkeep and repairs to the bar.

Two: April was never allowed to enter the upstairs apartments under

any circumstances.

April was too excited even to question the implications of both of these rules. At the moment, she considered them to be feasible enough. She began the renovation process with her vision of wanting guests to stay awhile and enjoy various forms of entertainment. A major bonus was that the basement was huge. The only things taking up any of the space in the basement were the breaker box and the water heater. These sat off in a far corner in a closeted area, taking up no space at all. If she could plan around that, this area could become whatever her heart desired. At that moment, she yearned to have a dance area. April converted the rather large basement of the bar into a club-like dance room. She wanted a place where women and men could dance, mingle, and find the love of their life if they were single. She was even envisioning the possibilities of a smaller bar area by the dance floor but paused, waiting to see if the dance floor idea would genuinely pay off.

It took a lot of work, no doubt, but April was fortunate to have many friends and family. These individuals all wanted to see her succeed. They pitched in wherever they could, which helped make the work never feel too overwhelming. Her son, Chris, worked hard breaking his back to help with the many aesthetic fixes, recreating the look and feel of his mom's new bar. April's daughter Nikki agreed to fill in to cook or with bartender duties. A few close friends, Tonya, Deanne, and Jennifer, trained to be her bartenders, as well.

On the main floor of the establishment, April added four large televisions. These sat high behind the bar anticipating busy Sunday Football Fundays. These TVs would come in handy throughout the year to feed every sports enthusiast. The next purchase was a pool table. It was strategically set up in the center of the main dining room to allow players to watch the TVs while they played pool. April also added a curiously popular golf arcade machine that future customers often requested before opening. To enhance the entertainment options, April knew how financially valuable it was to become involved with the gaming community of Plano. She immediately applied to offer five gaming machines. Once approved, she set them up in a row near the front entrance. Each one was different but a typical electronic slot machine. They seemed to offer decent payouts if one was patient enough to play for a while.

Fridays and Saturdays were going well. But during the week and once Sunday Football was over, she needed something more to pull in the crowd on the main floor. She knew just what she had to do, which immediately became her main attraction. Four electronic dart boards were all set up in the second room of the main floor. With customers always playing, she decided to coordinate an in-house dart league. She reached out to the local dart league coordinator, Randy. He assisted with preparing her boards for league play. The first league session was small and casual, but it helped increase the bar activities and profits.

April knew this league could grow but was concerned she would not have enough people to fill the teams. April reached out to her family and friends allowing her to create three teams for the league. She reached out to Randy for suggestions. Randy knew several local people who enjoyed playing darts and were looking for a place to play. The goal was to have eight teams, but with the help of Randy, there were nine three-player teams. The first night she started this session, players, supporters, and regulars packed the bar.

Typically each team would play another group on a rotating schedule every week. Eight teams would play every week while one team had a week off. With nine teams, there needed to be a bye-week. April decided to hold the league on her slowest day, Tuesdays. Due to friendly competition, the teams that had the bye week would often still show up, making April's busiest day of the week on Dart League Tuesdays. After three months of soft openings and minor repairs, she was finally ready to launch the grand opening of The 4/26. Even the local mayor and alderman had started to frequent her bar. Everything was coming together.

This Tuesday was a cause for true celebration because this would be the first Tuesday that dart league would take place officially in The 4/ 26. As you see, for many weeks, the Dart League players walked into the establishment that still showcased the Friendly's Tap signs, but now it was official. The 4/26 was officially ready to make an impact.

April had made friends with players on the other teams. Some of them reached out to help her expand her business. Notably, there was Drew and Becka, a couple who had managed to start up their own Karaoke business. With their budding friendship with April, Karaoke with Drew and Becka was now a thing every other Saturday. Drew and Becka's teammate Mikey, a lone female that always preferred her own company over others, would also join on Saturdays to sing a song or five.

A member of another team that April befriended was Zach. Zach's team consisted of two men who were twin brothers named after two members of the Beatles, George and Paul. Zach was an electrician with some HVAC experience. He began to help her (at a low cost, of course) repair a couple of electrical nightmares that would pop up from time to time. It is important to note that these electrical issues were primarily the cause of water damage seeping into her bar that traveled down from the second-floor apartments.

That water damage was the primary cause of April's concern. As April was not allowed upstairs, she could not know the extent of the problem in the apartments above her. She knew something had to be wrong because the water was now flooding into her bar every time it rained. The seeping rainwater was beyond frustrating because, with the bar on the first floor, rain reaching her bar from the second floor should not be possible. And yet, unfortunately, it became that every rainy day it was happening, and it was beginning to infuriate her. She had been in constant communication with her landlord, Zayan, and he empathetically promised her that he would fix the damages, but something happened that past Friday that changed everything. Zayan passed away in his sleep.

April had no personal disdain towards Zayan. She was genuinely saddened when she heard of his passing, even though it was not a significant shock when he passed at his age. However, April was also a little excited because Zayan's death meant she might have the opportunity to purchase the entire building. April envisioned the chance to start repairing whatever was going on upstairs without waiting for someone else to do it. But that would have to wait until later in the week because tonight was dart night, and Barb, her newly hired bartender, just showed up.

"You ready, dear?" April called out. "It is going to be busy."

Barb took off her sunglasses, looked at April, and answered, "Yeah, I am good, uhm you do know it is supposed to rain tonight, right?"

April brought a finger up to her lips and, in a whisper so none of the customers could hear, said, "Hush, I heard it might pass. Today is the official launch of The 4/26." April reached down and set two shot glasses down on the bar. She then reached behind her and grabbed a bottle of apple-infused whiskey, poured herself and Barb a shot, and said in a positively encouraging voice, "No jinxing us, okay?"

Barb walked over to the bar, grabbed her shot, and hesitantly said, "Of course."

April picked up her glass and held it high, exclaiming, "Okay then, to The 4/26!"

Barb smiled and cheered, "To The 4/26!"

Both women downed their shots and set their shot glasses on the bar. "Okay," April stated with determination. "Let's get to work. The teams should all start arriving shortly."

Just as they finished their prep work, the unmistakable sound of thunder rumbled outside. The storm seemed far enough to cause no concern but loud enough to catch April's attention. "Let's pray that whatever that was, passes," April hopefully said as she stepped from behind the bar. She made her way to the front door, ready to welcome her dart players and the other customers who were already starting to arrive.

Chapter 2: (2022) - Meet The Players

The Dart League didn't start until seven in the evening, but Cris and Laura always arrived thirty minutes prior. Their early arrival was for two reasons. One: Cris had a favorite dartboard that he enjoyed playing on, and Two: He also took those thirty extra minutes to practice and get into the "zone." Laura loved her husband, and since he technically was her ride, it did not bother her to be early. Cris was a competitive sort and had played darts in leagues before. Laura's health was failing her of late, so going out once a week to play darts was a sense of normalcy that she needed. It gave her a chance to socialize and forget about her woes for a few hours.

"Oh, look who is out to greet us!" Laura loudly exclaimed as Cris turned the corner onto Main Street. He pulled his truck into his usual parking spot across the street from the bar. Cris looked over and saw April standing at the bar's front door waving at them. Cris gave his typical slight little nod but could not find the will to wave back. He was under a lot of stress recently. Like most men often do, Cris kept his troubles bottled up inside. So much to the point that it could bubble over at times. But he had to keep his head in check. He had to look strong and, now more than ever, be strong for Laura.

Laura had been diagnosed with breast cancer two years prior. After multiple surgeries and treatments, she was often in good spirits. Cris, however, was understandably stressed. He worried about what was best for his wife but never wanted to tell her what to do. Nearly all of the patrons at the bar supported his wife and wished Laura well. Cris was grateful, but no one could understand what he was going through. The constant working, the continuous times he stayed up late at night praying for his wife's health to get better. No one knew the number of times he had cried alone, hidden away from everyone; He stubbornly had an image to maintain. The one thing everyone knew was that Cris would die and even kill for his wife.

"She better have a Red Apple!" Cris said with a laugh. Laura snickered as Cris put his truck into park. They gathered up their belongings, most importantly Cris's darts, and quickly made their way across the street towards the bar's front door.

"Hey guys," April called out as they walked towards the door.

"Hey to you," Cris hollered back, "You got Red Apple?"

"Of course," April gleamed as she turned and greeted Laura with a hug.

Cris walked past the two women and began to walk into the bar when he heard a low rumble of thunder. He turned and looked down the road and saw that the sky was starting to darken a long way off, possibly over the next town of Sandwich. "Is that going to stay over there?" he asked out loud.

"Oh, I hope so," answered April, trying to sound optimistic.

Cris shook his head with concern as he walked toward the bar. He knew it wasn't April's fault, but every time it rained, various areas of the ceiling inside of the bar leaked. When the rainfall was heavy or constant, a small flood would occur right inside her bar! What's worse is sometimes the leaks would impact both the ability to be served food and drinks, but to Cris, the most important of all, playing darts. The water fiasco could easily make the entire night unbearable. Cris was going to try and ignore it and keep his spirits up. Tuesday Night Dart League was his one night a week to have fun and escape his stress. He walked up to the bar, called out to Barb, and ordered a drink for himself and his wife.

As they turned the corner to locate a parking spot outside the bar, Becka smiled when she spotted April standing outside with Laura.

Becka waved at April. Drew informed Becka, "You know we play against her team tonight?"

Becka let out a loud, "Oh!" before scrunching up her face and sticking out her tongue. Her response caused Drew to laugh.

"You're such a dork," he smirked. Becka turned to him and batted her eyes. With a sing-songy tone, she replied, "And you're the one who loves me. So what does that make you?" Drew shook his head as he pulled into a parking spot directly in front of April's Mustang. He barely had the car in park before Becka had her door open and was starting to step out, leaving Drew to gather up their dart cases.

Becka thoroughly adored April. Together with her husband, Drew, she was determined to do whatever they could to help April's business succeed. Ironically, this friendship had one extraordinarily unusual and frustrating consequence. While Becka had befriended April, Drew had also developed a camaraderie with April's boyfriend, Joel. The two men created a friendly and sometimes annoying rivalry over professional football. Their friendly rivalry often led the two men to bet against the other's favorite teams. Unfortunately for Drew, his team typically did not fare well during the season, and Drew usually wound up on the wrong side of these bets. Becka loved Drew, but right now, he had his head shaved, one armpit waxed, and was now on the verge of getting his nipples pierced. He was her man, and she was going to stand by him, albeit begrudgingly, during their betting season.

Becka put a little bounce in her steps while approaching April and Laura. "Hey, girl, heeeyyy!" Becka called out as she got closer. April's eyes brightened as she laughed, tipping her head back. She stepped out of her spot at the doorway and onto the small step that led into the bar.

"Hey, girl!" April called out as she opened her arms to embrace Becka. Becka looked up at April and smiled; she then looked towards Laura and said, "Hey, how are you feeling?"

Laura returned the warm smile, "I am doing great!" Laura looked into the bar and said, "I'll let you two catch up and talk to you more inside." Laura made her way into the bar to join her husband.

Stacie and Ernie turned the corner just as Becka and April hugged each other. As Becka was about to follow Drew into the bar, Ernie rolled down the passenger window to yell out, "Hey, you two, get a room!" This, of course, elicited laughter from the two women and caused April to give him a friendly one-finger salute.

"She's gonna fucking kill you one day," Stacie laughed. Ernie laughed, replying, "Nah, that's your job." Stacie was in the grips of an insane laughing fit as she parked her white car next to Cris's truck. She loved Ernie to death. At that moment, it reminded her that she was pretty sure his laid-back attitude was one of the reasons why. Stacie and Ernie did not play on the same team. They could spend time together and have a guys/girls' night simultaneously.

"Who are you guys playing against?" Ernie asked.

"Here 4 the Beer," Stacie stated matter-of-factly.

"Oh shit," Ernie said, "That's Cris and Laura; damn, you guys are fucked."

"After a few drinks, it won't matter; we're here to have fun." Stacie smiled, thinking about what she was going to order first.

"I hear that, baby," Ernie said in a supportive tone. "We play April's kids' team, The Drunken Musketeers." Ernie overemphasized the team name with sarcastic finger quotes.

"They're pretty good," Stacie warned.

"We'll get 'em," Ernie answered confidently. "Me, Eric, and Billy will get it done."

"Speak of the devil," Stacie said as she pointed past Ernie. Ernie turned his head and saw that Eric and Billy both had arrived with their female companions. The ladies were Stacie's teammates, Hope, Eric's wife, and Lori, Billy's girlfriend.

Ernie stuck his hand out of his passenger window and called out, "You guys ready?"

"You know it!" Eric hollered back.

Billy started to jog a little towards the bar in true Billy fashion, leaving Lori behind. "Yeah! I am ready for a beer."

Ernie started to laugh and opened his car door. "Welp. Might as well get this thing started," he said as Stacie gathered up her purse and their dart cases.

Christian and his girlfriend, Lucy, saw Ernie get out of his car and waved at Eric. "Look, babe," Lucy laughed, "Billy is already running into the bar."

"Good," Christian said. "He is good, and the more he drinks the worse his throws."

"Not to mention the more money your mom will make." Lucy finished.

"No doubt," Christian said as he pulled into the parking spot in front of Drew and Becka's SUV. He waved over to Eric and Ernie, who was now crossing the street together. Stacie had met Laura and Hope on the opposite sidewalk to have a cigarette engaged in what looked to be a polite conversation. Christian turned back to Lucy, "You sure you're going to be okay, babe?" Lucy was not on a team this session but would support the League and Christian's mom, April, whenever her schedule allowed.

Lucy smiled up at Christian cheerily, "Yes. Sara is coming with Jason, so we will both have a good time cheering you guys on!" Chris smiled with relief and grabbed his dart case from the center console.

He stepped out of his car and heard his mother call out to him. "There's my Baby boy!" Christian rolled his eyes and walked over to his mom. "Mom, stop it," he said with a playful laugh.

Deanne and Mark turned onto Main Street from the opposite direction of everyone else. They lived in Lakewood, while most everyone else lived in the towns surrounding the bar, including

Sandwich. Jokingly, this made them the oddballs, but they didn't mind. They were both proud to be a little odd. Trying to quit smoking, Deanne was casually sucking on a blow pop. Mark smiled at his wife and, with a casually flirting way, "If you want something to suck on..." He teasingly pointed at his crotch. Deanne laughed loudly and slapped Mark on his shoulder. She then turned to look back out of the truck window.

Deanne was relieved and nervous. "God, my first night back and out of that damn cast!" Tonight was her first night back after breaking her ankle while tripping over her dog approximately six weeks prior. Not only was she glad to be free of the cast, but also happy to be back at the bar. Not only did she work there, but with the time spent and the friendships created, it was becoming her second home. Deanne saw two women she considered close friends standing outside the bar and began to wave excitedly towards them. Mark pulled the truck into a spot directly across the street from the bar. It was about a few cars down from Stacie's. As soon as their vehicle came to a complete stop, Deanne had her door open and nearly ran across the street to see Becka and April. Mark stared into his side mirror and shook his head while silently praying that his wife didn't trip over the curb, breaking her leg again. That would have been just their luck.

Holly pulled her car into a parking lot spot on the left side of the bar, facing the giant American flag mural that graced the windowless wall on the opposite side of the entrance to The 4/26. Her boyfriend, Dustin, also Laura's stepbrother, insisted they park there because it was hardly ever occupied. He was right, but Holly would never tell him so. It gave them a quiet and quick exit when they finished playing for the evening. "Is Kevin here?" Dustin asked.

"Uh, I dunno. I don't see his van?" Holly answered while trying to scan for the van. Kevin was their teammate, and if the bar had a designated clown, Kevin was it.

"I wonder what that goofy fucker is going to do tonight?" Dustin questioned with a laugh.

"Who knows," Holly sighed and laughed at the same time, rolling her eyes. But like Dustin, she was curious. Then almost as if he heard them, Kevin's van, which one could hear before even seeing it, came down the street. Kevin headed towards the spot he usually parked, right in front of the new collectible toy store that had just opened called Batcave Treasures.

"Welp, let's not keep 'em waiting," Dustin said as he opened his door.

Kevin put his van into park and looked over at the seat next to him. Tonight he was feeling a bit down; he had spent a good ten minutes sitting in his bathroom with his .45 wondering if today was going to be the day he put a bullet in his head. Kevin felt at his lowest as a recent divorcee and his mother's recent passing. Like always, he still found a reason to go on, his friends at the bar. But the gloom and feeling of rock-bottom still lingered strongly. Just in case he was finally through with it all tonight, the .45 was in the passenger seat, next to a bag of suckers and an old-style bicycle horn. Kevin's sense of humor was always on point as his mind worked faster than most. His quick wit, which could have a bite, was still always welcomed. Although he knew he was not very skilled at darts, he played to his strengths, currently the perfect distraction. Kevin gathered up his .45 still in its holster and tucked it into his waistband before gathering up his horn and stepping out of the van.

Mikey turned the corner just as Kevin stepped out of his van. She smiled when she saw Kevin with his horn. Mikey knew Kevin was a goof. She especially welcomed his positive attitude and joking behavior tonight, as she just found out her husband wanted a divorce. Mikey decided she would not stress about that tonight because Tuesday nights were all about having a few drinks and throwing darts. She slowly opened her vehicle door and heard Zach call out to her.

Zach lived within walking distance of the bar with his two roommates, George and Paul. The three were also teammates in the Dart League. Like most nights, Zach walked to the bar. It was the safest option because when he and his boys decided to drink, they drank! Tonight, however, Paul was not feeling it. Paul questioned as he gazed up into the gloomy night sky. "Dude, do you see those clouds? We should have driven."

"It'll be fine," Zach assured his friend as they crossed the street and began to make their way to the bar. "Besides, if it's too bad, someone will give us a ride." Zach noticed Mikey and yelled out, "Hey Mikey!" Paul and George waved back at Mikey just as Jason and his girlfriend, Sara, slowly drove past them. Jason leaned out his window and shouted out, "Get out of the road." At first, startled, the three men who stopped walking long enough to allow the couple to pass started laughing.

"Dude, we play them tonight, right?" Paul inquired.

"Nah, we play Kevin's team, and we are going to kick their ass!" Zach exclaimed with his fist shaking in pre-emptive victory.

The three men continued heading towards the door just as Kevin held the door open for Mikey. "Oh my hell does Kevin have a horn?' asked George as he gazed towards Kevin's hand.

"Holy shit!" Zach chuckled, "That motherfucker is going to create quite the scene tonight. I hope it distracts the other teams." Suddenly, a mild rumble of thunder rolled in, causing the men to quicken their pace towards the bar.

Jason and Sara pulled their car behind Kevin's van. "What are you and Lucy going to do tonight?" Jason questioned, trying to get a feel for what kind of mood Sara was in tonight.

"Probably play pool and watch you guys," Sara answered casually.

"Okay, babe," Jason replied with a feeling of relief as he opened his door.

"I don't want you getting bored." He was actually thinking that he didn't want to hear about her being bored later on in the night.

Sara smiled and reassuringly stated, "I think we will be fine; besides, did you see Kevin had a horn? There will be a lot for Lucy and me to watch and talk about."

Agreeing, Jason guffawed, "Yeah, April is probably gonna kill him, though; he's going to make her grand opening insane." The couple busted out laughing as they exited the car.

Jeremy and Brett arrived just in time to see Jason and Sara enter the bar. Although they rarely rode together tonight, Jeremy wanted to do a bit of drinking. He did not trust himself to drive after a night of celebration.

"Thanks, dude; I appreciate you picking me up," Jeremy said. Responded Brett, "No problem, man."

The two men sat in silence as Brett pulled his car into an available spot across the street from where Kevin had parked his van. The gentlemen exited the vehicle, and Brett looked up at the incoming clouds. The sky had grown even darker since he had picked Jeremy up about five minutes prior. "Shit! Looks like we're getting rained on tonight, heh heh."

"Don't jinx it," Brett quipped. But just as they began to cross the street, Brett felt a raindrop land on his cheek as another clap of thunder echoed through the darkening sky.

Chapter 3: 2022 - Round One Begins

Brett and Jeremy walked into the bar, marveling at just how much the place had changed since last Tuesday. What they thought would be only minor aesthetic changes, the renovation turned out to be so much more. Brighter bulbs replaced the previously low wattage dull ones. This simple change helped to make the place look more lively than ever. The dark shadows that once hung out in the far corners of the bar had been chased away by the renewed illumination. Although the bar was always well cleaned, April and her team had been busy. They had put in a lot of effort in the past week, and it showed. The only exception was a corner near a stack of chairs where Joel's tools were sitting, which was understandable. April had persuaded Joel to repair the physical damage on the ceiling. Sitting in the far corner was a circular saw, a toolbox, and for some reason, an ax. Assessing the construction taking place, Brett considered offering Joel the use of his reciprocating saw-saw, but his train of thought was interrupted by April.

"Yay, my team is here!" April shouted as she walked with a smile towards Jeremy, who was already making a beeline towards the bar. She gave Jeremy a brief hug. Jeremy, a relatively large, yet fit man, slightly lifted April off her feet before letting her go. "Hehe. Glad to be here, but I gotta get a drink before darts begin," he said as he let her go. April, smiling about how successful the night was turning out, approached Brett. The two exchanged a hug typical of fellow teammates before she asked him, "You ready?"

"Who are we playing?" Brett asked as he reached into his jacket and removed his dart case.

"Becka's team."April replied with a snarky sigh and partial grin.

Brett looked over and saw that Drew was already warming up. "Oh shit, this is going to be a tight game," he said with a half-smile, rolling his eyes.

"You know it. Let's hope they are off their game tonight. I mean, Becka can do good, but everyone else,well," April said with a mischievous grin.

Brett nodded and made his way over to the dart area. Greeted by Kevin, who for some reason was holding a horn in his left hand, Brett knew Kevin was up to one of his juvenile tricks. Kevin often did these antics to distract the opposing team's players, hopefully helping his team win. Quite honestly, no one really minded because Kevin did bring a new hilarity and goofy energy to the evening. It often helped to ease some of the stress from the competition. "You know if you get better at throwing, you wouldn't have to use shit like that," Brett dryly told Kevin as the two shook hands.

"Hey, I'm trying," Kevin said with a laugh, holding up his hands in self-defense. "But the game is half mental, and we are playing Zach and the twins."

Brett winced," Oh yeah, the twins are dangerous opponents when they are on their game; you might need that horn. Just don't blow it in my direction while I am throwing." Kevin nodded in agreement before excusing himself to go to the bar.

Brett looked around and noticed that all the teams had already selected the boards they were playing on. The dartboards lined the back wall and were number one through four from left to right. There was just enough spacing between them so the players could comfortably maneuver around each other. The first dartboard was near the second entrance to the bar. This board just so happened to be Cris and Laura's favorite. One of the reasons they showed up early was so they could lay claim to that board. No one typically cared because everyone firmly believed in the "first come, first serve" rule. Here 4 the Beer was the name of Cris, Laura, and their partner, A.J.'s team. Tonight they were up against The Lady Bulls, which consisted of Stacie, Hope, and Lori.

Kevin's team, Scripted Intentions, included Holly and Dustin. Kevin selected their team name since he was a player in the previous dart league session. Since Kevin was at the bar first tonight, he chose the second dartboard. Their opposing team, Beer B4 Bulls, had no qualms with the board choice. That team consisted of Zach, George, and Paul. They liked Kevin enough, and although he was a bit odd and awkward, everyone got along very well.

Now there was an unspoken rule about the third dartboard. Everyone knew of this rule, and traditionally everyone followed it. Given any possibilities, April's team would play on dartboard number three. Brett walked over and set his dart case down next to April's. He hugged Becka and waved to Mikey, sitting at the table next to them. Brett was playing against their team. April had named their team "We are 4-26," which was fitting, he guessed, as he was representing the bar's owner every time he stepped up to throw a dart. Drew, Becka, and Mikey went under the insane team name of "2 Chix and a Dick," although a tad immature, the name was very fitting considering Drew's playful humor.

The fourth and final dartboard was next to the door leading to April's smoking deck positioned behind the bar. This fourth board was the least desired board because people constantly interrupted the game to go in and out. The Drunken Musketeers, consisting of Christian (April's son), Robby, who was running late that night, and Jason, had to play on that board. They were playing against Ernie, Eric, and Billy, who poetically named their team The Dirtbags.

Deanne, her husband Mark, and their friend Sherri made up the ninth team. Aptly named The Darts of Hazard, it had a bye-week. Mark and Deanne sat at the center tables hoping Sherri would join them shortly. The tables nestled between boards two and three, almost like a divider. Even though they were not playing this week, they showed up to cheer everyone on with moral support. Of course, since she did work there, Deanne couldn't miss the official The 4/26 celebration.

Brett smiled, realizing that he was in for a good night. He reached into his pants pockets, pulled out his AirPods, and placed them in his ear. Brett turned on his phone, searching for the right song. Once he found the right piece to get him started, he waited for the world to go quiet. He took his last opportunity to practice before the league began.

A.J. knew he was late, but it's not as if Cris and Laura had anything to do tomorrow. He had just worked a long shift, but being true to his word, A.J. was going to be there for his team. Slowly he pulled his car into a parking spot. He opened the door immediately as he shut off his engine. He smiled in relief when he saw Robby turn the corner. A.J. felt better knowing he was not the only one who was late.

There was a slight amount of rainfall; one might call it a drizzle, but whatever the case, the rain was never a good thing when it came to The 4/26. Robby was in a hurry while also a bit concerned. As he stepped outside, he hurriedly ran back into his house. Robby figured he should grab his wet vac and a couple of buckets just in case. He knew he was going to be late, but he had a feeling these things might come in handy. Robby breathed a sigh of relief when he saw A.J. getting out of his car. Instead of parking in front of the building, Robby turned the next corner and pulled his vehicle onto the small grassy area beside the smoking deck. He figured this was a wise choice if he had to run out and get the stuff in his car. The smoking exit was faster and easier than the available parking spots. Quickly he gathered up his darts and sweatshirt and made his way inside.

Jennifer, Tanya, and April's daughter, Nikole, showed up together. All three were bartenders at the bar, but tonight was their night off. Even though these ladies appreciated the Dart League members, they were not there specifically to cheer them on. These three were there to check out the new dance room April had set up downstairs. Aware April had not yet finished the dance room, they still knew it would be a fun time. The woman slowly walked into the bar as Nikole's mother, April, immediately approached her. "Niki!" April exclaimed. April ran over to her daughter, arms outstretched. Nikole smiled as she saw her mother run over. She opened her arms and let out a high-pitched childish, "Mom!" and hugged her mother.

"You guys here to check out the dance floor?" April asked.

"Yes, ma'am!" Tanya interjected with a Midwestern/Southern accent.

April smiled, "Alright, girls, you guys go have fun; Candy and Michelle may be coming too, but the bar down there isn't quite ready. I can see if Deanne will run drinks down for you guys!"

"Okay, mom," Nikole said, and the three women hurried towards the basement stairs to see the transformation of the basement.

April gleamed as she watched her daughter go into the basement. She stood there for a couple of seconds, taking it all in, as the past few weeks were indeed hard work. But April had no time for that right now. Her establishment was bustling. Almost all of the Dart League players were there, a couple of regulars that had filtered in seated at the bar, and an older man everyone called Paco. Soon, three blue-collar guys who always showed up after work to unwind, Kyle, Kory, and Danny, moseyed in. As April was about to turn around to start playing darts, she heard the bell over her door ring out. Sherri walked in, closely followed by Candy and Michelle. Tonight was going to be a good night; she just knew it.

April was lost in her train of thought and would have stayed there for a bit if it weren't for Jeremy's loud booming voice echoing through the bar. "April, we're starting; get over here!" He shouted. April quickly snapped out of her reverie, smiled, and walked over to the dartboards. It was time to play, and she was determined to show Drew, Becka, and Mikey that she could shoot darts with the best of them. When April arrived at the boards, she saw that everyone had already put their ten dollars into the machines. Cris was already throwing his first dart.

Dustin, who was shooting first for Kevin's team, was in the process of stepping up to the oche, or toe line, that was precisely eight feet away from the dartboard. Ernie was preparing to throw for his team. April walked over and opened her dart case. Jeremy had already put ten dollars in for her, and she was up first.

"Sorry guys," April said as she hurried to the oche, "I was saying hi to my baby."

"It's okay, April, we understand," Becka began saying supportively but quickly turning it into the friendly trash-talking the players shared. "You're scared; we get it."

"Oh hell no," April remarked with a laugh. "Tonight, we're going to beat your ass!" Becka burst out laughing in response. April, still smiling, stepped up on the line. Just as she positioned her toe and lifted her arm, a loud rumble of thunder ripped through the air. It was so powerful the thunder caused shaking inside the first-floor bar. April's smile vanished as quickly as the thunder rolled in.

Chapter 4: (1975 through 1979) - The Child Grows

Zeus grew accustomed to his new life. Zayan kept to his weekly visits and did not interact much with the child. Instead, he only provided toys or learning supplies. Zayan never once pretended to be anything other than the delivery guy, avoiding eye contact with his son. Being only three, Zeus did not have much of a memory of his mother. The only person Zeus knew as a parent was his caretaker, Patricia. True to her word, Patricia cared and raised Zeus as if he was her own. Patricia wanted to keep Zeus safe. She convinced the boy that the world would persecute and destroy him, causing Zeus to develop agoraphobia quite early. By the time Zeus was five, he had no desire to look out the windows. Patricia was quite relieved by this.

Patricia knew that the child's existence would be a sad one indeed. She assumed that Zeus would be persecuted and bullied based on his appearance even if the world outside would not physically destroy him. Her job was to keep him safe and in one place. Patricia, though, was happy with her new arrangement. While she taught Zeus to fear the world outside, she despised it. Patrica hated people, primarily men, but she could easily live her daily life without people.

Patricia was not an unattractive woman; every man she met was only interested in "one thing." While Patricia did enjoy that "one thing" when she was willing, she found the need for a partner useless once she discovered alternative forms of physical pleasure. Patricia further distanced herself from people. She needed money, and while she did not have a college degree nor did she belong to a higher class of society, most of the jobs available to her were retail or restaurant work. While those jobs required some degree of social interaction, they often led to her termination. Like many women at that age, Patricia's biological clock began ticking. She was starting to yearn for a child. But again, that would require her to seek out male companionship. As luck would have it, she came across Zayan's ad in the paper, leading her to where she is now, raising a child while staying far away from society.

Zeus turned out to be very intelligent. At age four, using simple tinker toys and an erector set that Patricia had requested, Zeus built an elaborate tower capable of constant motion. A small buck would travel up and down this tower to deliver a marble that would race down a track. The bucket would catch the marble as it dropped and raised to the top of this tower once again, where it repeated the entire process.

Using books that Zayan had acquired from local school supply warehouses, Patricia began to teach the boy basic mathematics, reading, and science. Zeus took to his teachings like a fish to water. Before long, he was reading and solving problems that could pose a challenge for children over half his age. This did not surprise Patricia because while the boy was not much to look at, she knew that the good Lord did not make him an idiot either. She knew something was special about the child. She properly rewarded every showing of intelligence and act of genius.

Zeus, like most children, had taken a fondness for sweets. Patricia, a very crafty woman in the kitchen, baked him several assorted goodies whenever the boy exceeded her expectations. As often as Zeus impressed her, Patricia requested that Zayan bring in large amounts of premade snack cakes and toys to avoid overworking herself in the kitchen.

Zeus, though, didn't need the incentives to learn. He legitimately enjoyed learning everything: mathematics, literature (both fictional and historical), but his true passion was science. Everything involving science was something that grasped Zeus's immediate attention. By the time his fifth birthday arrived, he was requesting everything from microscopes to building blocks to try and build something that would test the limits of his imagination.

Zeus had just turned six, and the lovely man who visited his home once a week left behind a brand new state-of-the-art microscope along with a box of small bricks that snapped together. He was absolutely in love with the bricks. Patricia watched him play while Zeus snapped those bricks together with ease and enthusiasm. In no time, he had built a rather odd-looking contraption. As you may recall, he only had two digits on either hand, making his building skills even more impressive. Before long, Zeus's interests went from the bricks to the microscope. A couple of months before the decade's end, Zeus discovered something that took him entirely by surprise and revealed a unique talent that he didn't know he had.

The new microscope was not small, designed to magnify things nearly a hundred times more than the ones he had prior. When he put the slide containing a wing of a butterfly on the stage section of the microscope, Zeus trembled in anticipation as he knew there was going to be something new for him to discover. The image of the wing popped. It was more vibrant than anything he had ever seen before. The colors were almost indescribable. Zeus was awestruck by the beauty he had missed by his smaller, weaker telescope. He excitedly started to change the slides but paused as he heard something.

It was a low voice, barely above a whisper. Zeus could have sworn it was saying, "Look at us."

Puzzled, he looked down at the small wooden box that housed roughly twenty slides.

"Us, look at us," the voice came again.

A typical child might have thrown the box across the room and run away screaming, but Zeus was not any ordinary child. Wanting to discover whatever he was hearing, he began to pull the slides out of his box, one at a time. Zeus held each one close to his ear. Slide by slide, each one was silent. For a moment, he thought maybe he was going crazy. Unexpectedly, on the ninth slide labeled MOLD, he heard the voices, "Look at us!"

He had looked at the mold before; it was nothing too special. With his new microscope and hearing voices, he had to look again. Zeus put the slide on the microscope stage. This time under better magnification, what he saw could only be described as frightening. The image sent chills up and down his spine. The mold was slowly moving in a circular pattern, swirling. Zeus concluded that this small batch of what should have been inert mold was very much alive.

"Do you see us?" The mold implored.

Zeus hesitated before answering, "Yes."

"Can you free us?" the mold pleaded.

Zeus sat back, pulling himself away from the ocular lens. 'Free us?' he thought to himself. What could that mean? He took a deep breath and once again looked through the ocular lens at the living mold. "What do you mean free you?" Zeus asked gingerly.

The mold hissed, "From this prison. Set us to someplace wet, dark."

Zeus pulled himself away from the microscope before looking around his room. He saw a towel on his floor that he had used after taking his bath this morning. Zeus walked over to the towel. He reached down to pick it up and felt that it was still damp. Zeus carried the towel over to the microscope. Carefully removing the mold slide, he placed it on top of the towel. Using the extended nail on his digit that most resembled a thumb of a normal hand, Zeus peeled back the small piece of vinyl that covered the sentient mold sample. He rubbed the mold on the towel before scanning his room once more. He noticed that his bed was exceptionally dark underneath as it was only about six inches off the ground. Zeus got on his hands and knees and pushed the towel far under his bed.

"Thank you," the mold uttered graciously.

"No problem," Zeus happily replied.

Zeus continued to bring cups of water into his room to help keep the towel damp. Before he knew it, the small amount of mold had grown into a much larger-sized patch on the towel. Zeus continued to care for the mold. He would communicate with it almost as if the mold were a pet.

One day as Patricia passed by his bedroom door, she heard Zeus talking in his room, but she was unsure what he was saying. She opened his door. Zeus was lying half off of his bed with his head hanging off it. He appeared as if he was looking at something underneath his bed. "How are you doing?" Patricia heard Zeus ask.

"Dear, who are you talking to?" she asked him with concern in her voice.

Apparently, she startled him because Zeus sat straight up while looking at Patricia with wide, fearful eyes. "M-m-my friends," he stammered.

Patricia smiled. Observing this moment of normalcy from a child that most would call a freak warmed her heart. Having imaginary friends was utterly ordinary. "Okay, dear," she warmly responded, "but you need to wrap it up. You have to read soon."

"Okay, Mama Patricia," Zeus called out.

Patricia gleamed as she brought her hand up to her chest. Zeus had never called her Mama; hearing him say that brought a tear to her eye. She did not bother correcting him. Instead, she lovingly told him, "You can just call me Mama." Patricia dropped her hand to her side, "You have fifteen minutes to say goodbye to your friend. I expect to see you in the living room reading." She excused herself and left Zeus to continue talking to his friends, not knowing what was really under Zeus's bed.

Chapter 5: 2022 - A Fatal Low Ton

As soon as the thunder reverberated off the walls of the bar, April winced. It sounded like the storm was practically on top of them, which concerned her. Her first thought was if the roof started leaking, it would ruin the night. Tonight was supposed to be perfect, and now it looked like the weather wanted to destroy a great time.

Robby jumped out of his seat and walked out the smoking area's door. He jogged slowly over to his car, where he proceeded to collect the wet vac and buckets he had decided to bring just in case the weather did turn for the worst. He stopped and looked around and noticed the sky was thick with clouds. The storm was right on top of them. At any moment, it was going to unleash a downpour onto the town of Plano.

Meanwhile, Jeremy was still inside. He noticed April's distraction and what looked like a depressed demeanor. Jeremey approached April as she was still standing on the marker, preparing to throw her first dart. He put his arm around her shoulder and, in a supportive teammate fashion, told her, "You got this, and don't worry, we got you."

April looked up at Jeremy and smiled before patting him on his chest and nodding in agreement. She then looked at the board, took a deep breath, and threw her first dart. As April's dart hit the board, Robby walked in, carrying the wet vac and buckets. Without saying a word, he walked past his team. They looked at him with visible confusion as he handed the items to Barb. "When it starts raining, put the buckets under the biggest leaks."

Robby was Barb's paramour; they were undercover lovers. There was a certain spark, a connection between the two. One would only notice if they were watching them at the very moment he smiled at her while she nodded her head. Robby, wanting to help her in any way he could, had informed Barb about the leaks in the bar. Barb knew what she had to do if the storm hit. That would help her make a great first impression in April. After exchanging their last smiles for the moment, Robby hurried back over to his teammates.

"Dude, did you just bring in a vacuum cleaner?" Jason asked.

"A wet vac," Robby corrected, "and yeah, just in case it floods somewhere, we can use that to suck up some of the water."

"Cool," Jason responded as he realized it was now his turn.

April had finished throwing her darts and had scored a modest eighty-five points for her team. She had overheard Jason and Robby's conversation and smiled at Robby as she went over to pick up her beer. Robby just nodded at her showing her he understood. Everyone continued taking turns with only mild rumbles of thunder sounding off outside. April started to relax and was smiling. She even started laughing when she heard Kevin shout out, "Holy shit, we won one!"

Kevin's team was not the best in the league, but they still knew how to have fun. Kevin was lucky this session as his team was not at all the worst. They were doing pretty well, thanks to Holly, who was almost always on target. Dustin was decent, but sometimes his competitiveness got into his head, causing him to make rookie mistakes. It was Kevin's antics that helped to drive his team forward. Whether it was his jokes or props, Kevin always made people laugh. Even if you were playing against him, you couldn't help but have fun. April noticed the horn Kevin had brought in and thanked God she wasn't playing against him. She would have strangled him if he honked the horn at her, but she couldn't wait until he did it to someone else. Since Kevin's team had just won the first round, the horn currently sat on the table, silent. Cris, however, was far from quiet. The whole bar knew that his team was winning. "Fuck yeah!" echoed throughout.

Cris was insanely competitive, and every time he scored a low ton or higher, he could be heard yelling "FUCK YEAH" out at the top of his lungs. April laughed hearing this because she had never seen someone so into darts as Cris. Laura had her own thing as well. Every time she scored high, she would yell out a loud "Woot Woot" that nearly sounded like a police siren. A.J. was not as boisterous, but his British accent would always steal the spotlight. Stacie's team was not playing very well this session. The women only played this session to get out of the house and spend time with their significant others. They were officially in last place, and tonight they were facing Cris, Laura, and A.J., who may have been the best team. Stacie was on her third beer and second game when Cris loudly called out, "Fuck yeah!"

"Yay," Stacie smiled while rolling her eyes. "You got the darts to go where they were supposed to." Her sarcasm drew laughter from Hope and Laura. Cris smiled and jokingly stuck his tongue out at her. The ladies were still laughing when Kevin reached over for his horn.

Brett noticed Kevin and immediately tapped Drew on the shoulder as he was fixing to throw a dart. Although Brett was playing against Drew's team, he didn't want Drew to miss a chance for a good throw. Brett wanted to win fair and square.

Deanne took notice. She had been the one who initially invited Kevin to play darts in the league. They knew each other because Kevin's son rode the bus Deanne drove before becoming a bartender. She nudged her husband, who was talking to Sherri. Mark looked up and did his best to stifle a giggle.

Mikey noticed and said, "Oh shit," and leaned close to Becka. "He's doing it," she whispered.

By now, everyone had noticed Kevin had the horn in his hand. Everyone except for George, that is. George was too busy focusing on where to put his next dart. No one moved. Kevin, who knew he was now the focal point of attention at this juncture, was either going to have to honk the horn or let everyone down. He shrugged, and just as Georgie prepared to throw his dart, Kevin squeezed the bulb of his noisemaker.

A loud honk sounded throughout the bar. George somewhat jumped as he let go of his dart. The dart flew high and in the fat wedge zone of the one. George turned around and looked at Kevin.

"Asshole!" he called out, clearly on the verge of laughing.

Instead of saying a word, Kevin just honked the horn again. His antics brought another round of laughter from everyone in the bar. Immediately, the unmistakable sound of rain hitting the roof filled the bar, stifling the laughter.

"Shit!" April growled in frustration as she folded her arms and laid her head down on the table.

Robby walked over to the bar as soon as the rain started. He could tell the rain outside was getting heavier. "Barb!" he called out. "Gimme the buckets!" He rushed, well for Robby, it was rushing, over to Kyle, Kory, and Danny. They were seated near the slot machines at the end of the bar. The three men watched Robby approach them as Barb set the buckets on the bartop. Robby quickly grabbed the buckets and handed one to each of the men. Swiftly depleting the stack of buckets he brought, they were down to just one left. "You guys know where to put them" was all he said.

As Kyle, Kory, and Danny began to set up buckets preparing to catch the trespassing rainwater, Ernie called out, "Hey, might as well take a smoke break." And with that, he and Billy walked out the door towards the smoker's area, effectively pausing their game.

As Kevin looked over at April, his heart dropped a little. He wanted her bar to succeed, but there was a long road for her to travel. "It can't rain all the time," he mumbled under his breath.

"What?" Holly asked while looking at him, confused.

Kevin shook his head, "Nothing."

"Well, it's your turn," Dustin said," And until April says so or the roof caves in the games still go on."

There was a loud collective "Hell yeah!" Cris, Kevin, and Becka all stepped up to the toe line to take their turns. The teams on the fourth dartboard were in limbo, waiting for the guys to come back in from smoking.

Now satisfied with the three regulars' work, Robby decided to step outside and join Ernie and Billy for a smoke. He passed by April's table and saw that April's head was down. He shook his head and put his hand on her shoulder. He leaned in close and whispered, "It's ok; we got you."

April raised her head. Robby could tell that she had been holding back tears. "Thank you," was all that she could mutter at the moment.

Robby, smiling, gave her shoulder one more squeeze before he turned to go outside to have a cigarette.

Water had started slowly dripping into the bar. Thankfully Robby had Kory, Kyle, and Danny set up buckets in the locations where the water dripped the heaviest. Barb had already retrieved the mop bucket and dry mop, setting it close to the edge of the bar, hoping to catch any other wayward leaks that may happen to spring up now and then. There was one leak that no one even knew about, even with all of their hard work and preparation.

A small leak had formed behind the second dartboard, where Kevin, Dustin, and Holly played. Shadows from the dartboard that cast up towards the ceiling concealed the small trickle of rainwater that flowed down. It began to form a puddle underneath the base of the dartboard. No one noticed the hazardous situation unfolding as everyone focused on Kevin surprisingly having the best game of his life.

The wind had picked up, rattling the door next to Cris, causing him to stop playing just before Kevin threw his first dart. Cris turned towards Laura while watching Kevin throw a bullseye with his first dart. Cris knew Kevin was not that great of a dart player. Kevin did have the luck of the draw when he was in the zone. That was when Kevin could put up some excellent points. No one was more surprised than Kevin himself when he did well. It was always entertaining to watch his borderline goofy celebrations.

Robby hurriedly walked outside, nearly knocking over Billy as he rushed back inside. "Screw that," Billy grumbled as he hurried past, "That wind is a son of a bitch."

Robby smiled and looked over to see Ernie huddled in a far corner smoking. Robby dug out his cigarettes and stepped onto the small patio built by April and Joel, allowing people to smoke. He felt the wind instantly, but like most addicts, he needed a cigarette, and he was going to have one.

Turning his back to the wind, Robby dug out his lighter. After finding a place where he felt he could light his cigarette, he brought his lighter to life and inhaled deeply. Robby then walked over to join Ernie in the back of the patio. In the back corner, it seemed mainly sheltered from the wind.

"Nice fucking weather, huh?" Ernie snickered.

Robby took another deep drag, "Yeah, poor April, though. This is a fucked up way to start a grand reopening."

Ernie silently nodded in agreement.

When Billy walked inside, he stopped and saw everyone focused on Kevin. Kevin started laughing nervously. Billy looked over at Eric and asked, "What's going on?"

With a smile on his face, Eric replied, "Kevin threw two bulls and is one dart away from a hat trick."

"Oh, no shit? Is that right?" Billy craned his neck over to watch for himself.

Hat tricks were uncommon. Only the more seasoned and damn near professional players could score one. Three bullseyes were all one needed to earn a hat trick. Kevin was lucky to hit the bullseye three times in an entire thirteen-game sequence and was now just one dart away. Cris walked over to Kevin, "Relax, bud, you got this. You get it, and I'll get you a beer."

Kevin nodded and threw his last dart. From where Kevin stood, it looked like it was on track. Kevin cringed when his third dart sailed low, falling slightly and sticking into the lower wedge of the nineteen scoring section. Although he did not earn a hat trick, 119 points were not too shabby. The bar let out a collective "Aww," except for Becka. She yelled out her signature phrase, "Nice motherfuckin' low ton!"

Kevin turned and bowed before walking over to get his darts. As he approached the board, he noticed the screen on the front that showed everyone the score flickered for a moment, but he thought nothing of it. He reached up and grabbed his first dart by the metal barrel, and suddenly everything went to hell.

The water had pooled behind the dartboard and began shorting it out. Water then started seeping out from underneath the dartboard's base. This particular dartboard operated at a high amperage. Kevin approached the dartboard, completely unaware of the water that had puddled in front of it. He unknowingly stepped into the water and the moment he touched his dart barrel, the current jumped into Kevin's body, instantly electrocuting him.

Kevin's body immediately tensed up like stone. His eyes went wide, and his body convulsed wildly. Kevin had a strange habit of placing the tip of his tongue between his teeth when he concentrated. As hundreds of volts surged through his body, and every muscle tightened up for dear life, his jaw slammed shut, violently slicing his tongue in two.

At first, everyone thought Kevin was only messing around. A few laughs came from the crowd that watched the darts tournament. Someone called out, “Nice try, asshole; give it up already!” That was when Zach noticed white foam mixed with blood leaking from the corners of Kevin's mouth. The acrid smell of frying bacon and burnt hair suddenly filled the bar. Zach, who was a licensed electrician and HVAC technician, immediately recognized what was happening.

"Holy fuck!" Zach gasped as he pointed, "Kevin's being electrocuted!"

George and Paul jumped up and rushed to help Kevin, but Zach stopped them. "No, no, don't touch him," he warned, "you'll get shocked too."

The lights began to flicker as Kevin's body started to sizzle. Cris grabbed Laura and pulled her toward him, averting his eyes from the gruesome sight. He couldn't bring himself to watch Kevin die. Everyone ran into the bar's central area, except for Dustin and Billy, who appeared to be entranced by the horrific scene unfolding before their very eyes.

Suddenly, Dustin called out, "Kevin!" But there was no answer.

Mikey and Becka were in the main bar area, holding tight to each other, trying not to cry. Eric held Hope's head against his chest as she began to sob. Lori and Stacie hurriedly tiptoed around the scene and into the far corner of the bar, covering their ears and holding their breath. Holly closed her eyes and began to pray. Everyone else turned away as no one wanted to watch Kevin die.

April ran over to the bar and screamed at Barb to cut the main power switch on the bar's breaker box. Barb was frozen in place, completely stunned at the appalling sight of Kevin's now smoking body still standing in front of the dartboard. Drew recognized that Barb was in shock and quickly jumped over the bar. He dashed to the breaker box with Jeremy and April's son, Christian, close behind him. Just then, Jason made his way over to the women's bathroom, where Lucy and Sara were walking out with their hands up, confused by the commotion. They had no clue what had happened.

"Stay right there!" Jason demanded, "Kevin is being electrocuted."

Lucy's eyes went wide, "What?" She asked as she frantically glanced around the bar, searching for Christian.

Kory, Kyle, and Danny jumped up to their feet to see if they could help their friend. When they approached the darts area, the smell of burning flesh was so thick they started to gag and began stumbling backward away from the horrid scene. Deanne, Mark, A.J., and Sherri had fled the darts area, rushing over to Holly to join her in prayer.

Curiously, Dustin never moved. Billy ran over and grabbed Dustin by the shoulder. "Come on, man!" Billy pleaded, trying to pull Dustin away from the darts area, "no one needs to see this." Dustin stood there watching as if he were comatose. The skin around Kevin's hand started to turn black. The charing began to make its way down Kevin's arm and the smell of burnt hair was even more putrid now. Dustin tried desperately to make himself turn away, but could not. It was as if he was watching a train wreck happening right in front of him.

Now Kevin's head was starting to smoke. Fresh blood trickled from his ears and eyes as his hair began falling from his scalp. The hair collected in singed and ashy piles at his feet in the puddle that had now all but evaporated. At that moment, Drew found the breaker box and flipped the switch marked 'main power'. The bar went dark and a loud thud came from the darts area. When the current broke, Kevin's body hit the floor. Assuming all was safe, Drew flipped the main power switch back on. Just as he did, a loud chorus of screams came from the basement where the group of girls were dancing.

Paco, the old man who had been in the bathroom the entire time, stepped out, and in his drunken state shouted, "Who the fuck is burning bacon?!"

Then the entire building started to vibrate.

Chapter 6: 2022 - What's in the Basement?

Nicole, Jennifer, Tanya, Candy, and Michelle had gathered at the bar just as everyone started to get ready to play darts. They passed by Lucy and Sara, who were playing pool.

"You ladies want to see what my mom has done to the basement?" Nikole excitedly squealed to the two girls.

"Sure," Sara shrugged with a smile.

"We'll meet you down there after we're done with our game and go to the bathroom!" Lucy chimed in while focusing on her next shot.

Each of the five women walked over to the bar to grab some drinks. When Barb had given Michelle, the last one to order, her beer, April was throwing her first dart. The ladies started to make their way into the basement.

When Nikole stepped onto the basement floor, she was impressed by what her mother had accomplished. Gone was the cold concrete slab. Instead, a beautiful and inviting hardwood floor shined. Over to the left on the far wall were four tables, each with four sets of chairs. The lighting was low but well-lit enough to see just how much April had done. Hanging from the ceiling was a retro disco ball bringing a smile to Nicole's face and a giggle from Candy.

Nikole had the app installed on her phone, so she started it up and opened it. Three prominent speakers are suspended from the ceiling, while on the right wall is a new-style jukebox that one could access with their cell phone. The jukebox itself was no bigger than a T.V. screen and required a strong internet connection to access the plethora of songs from the jukebox company's digital database. It was pretty similar to the one April had installed upstairs, only slightly smaller. Several surrounding bars had similar jukeboxes installed, and the app could link to all of them. Nikole selected The 4/26 as her location and highlighted Jukebox #2. In seconds, a loud booming hip hop song about female empowerment began to flow from the speakers.

The music was loud but not too loud. The girls could hear themselves speak just fine, and the concrete floor above their heads probably prevented the music from being heard upstairs. Nikole sauntered over to the table where the ladies set their drinks and waved her arms in the air. "Woohoo! Who's ready to dance?" She called out very bubbly and high-pitched.

Candy had been swaying from side to side in time with the beat. She reached over and grabbed Michelle by the hand and dragged her into the middle of the makeshift dance floor. Michelle feigned resistance at first before laughing and dancing while walking with Candy. Tanya stood in place and began to laugh as she slowly started to clap her hands. Tanya knew that she did not have the gift of rhythm, but she was here for a good time. Tanya could care less what anyone thought of her. She folded her arms above her head and slowly shook her hips as she, too, made her way onto the dance floor. Jennifer had pulled out a chair and sat down.

"Oh no, no, no!" Nikole exclaimed as she walked over and took Jennifer's hand. "We are dancing, girl!"

"Ugh!" Jennifer moaned in annoyance. "Let me have a few drinks first, okay?" She looked up at Nikole, who was sticking out her upper lip in an exaggerated version of a frown. "Oh, stop it! I will dance in a minute, okay!?" Jennifer suddenly saw something that made her look past Nikole. In the far shadows where the maintenance closet housing the water heater, furnace, and downstairs breaker box, Jennifer watched as the door slowly opened, seemingly on its own.

"What the hell?" Jennifer cried out loudly.

Nikole noticed that Jennifer was looking past her and turned around just in time to see what looked like a long black tendril slither out of the now open doorway momentarily before quickly sliding back inside the maintenance closet, closing the door behind it.

Jennifer jumped to her feet. "Holy shit, did you just fucking see that?"

"Uh yeah, I did," Nikole responded with her eyes open in a mix of surprise, confusion, and fear.

"Was that a fucking snake?" Jennifer asked.

"I don't know," Nikole remarked. "A snake getting into the basement is possible, I suppose" Nikole had never seen a snake that dark in color or with the ability to close a door, but that part of the basement had barely any light. The shadows could have been playing tricks on them. "I'll check it out," Nikole stuttered bravely.

"Be careful," Jennifer pleaded as Nikole started walking towards the maintenance room door.

Meanwhile, the other three women continued dancing, utterly oblivious to what was happening.

Nikole cautiously made her way to the maintenance door. Candy was the first of the three dancing women to notice. Nikole walking over to the maintenance room wasn't alarming in itself, but it was the way she was walking. Nikole, unaware that she was doing it, was slightly hunched over with her head sideways as she slowly crept towards the door. She was trying her best to move stealthily. Candy giggled and tapped Tanya on the shoulder, directing her to look at Nikole. Michelle noticed Nikole on her own, and suddenly all three women watched as Nikole crept up on the maintenance room.

Jennifer walked up to the trio and nervously said, "We saw a snake."

Candy, who was deathly afraid of snakes, cringed, "For real?"

"Well, we saw something?" Jennifer stated, almost as if she was questioning herself.

"What's Nikole doing?" Michelle asked.

Tanya snickered, "Looks like she's trying to sneak up on it like a kitten ready to pounce."

The four women then fell silent as Nikole arrived at the door. With a trembling hand, she reached up and turned the doorknob slowly. Just then, the lights began to flicker as if they were teasing to shut off. Nikole held onto the doorknob, not realizing she was holding her breath. She pulled the door and swung it open. The lights instantly went out.

The lights were out for just a moment, although it felt like an eternity. They were off long enough for something to strike Nikole hard in the chest, sending her sprawling backward. When the lights clicked back on, Nikole, along with the rest of the women, saw what looked like a long black snake rising out of the maintenance room. In the middle of the maintenance room, Nikole looked past the "thing." She noticed the base of whatever was in front of her was rising out of the floor drain. Nikole gaped at the head of whatever had hit her and realized there were no eyes, mouth, or anything resembling what could belong on the face of an animal. It was just a swirling black tendril of what appeared to be filth. Nikole did the only thing she could do at that moment.

She screamed.

Nikole's screaming broke the paralysis that had gripped the other four women, and they too started screaming. That is when the entire building began to shake above them. The enormous black snake-looking thing retreated and disappeared into the floor drain with a loud, wet-sounding swoosh noise just as the building shook.

Tanya quit screaming long enough to shout out, "What the fuck is happening?"

Nikole scrambled to her feet as the sounds of loud crashing and splintering wood resonated above them. She glanced back at the maintenance room and saw the snake was gone. Nikole ran over and joined the women on the dance floor, huddled together in the center of the dance floor.

The noise above them grew louder. The women feared that the floor above them would collapse at any moment and bring the entire bar area and its patrons down on their heads. The building shook for a full five minutes before it stopped. The loud crashes and thuds above them soon stopped, too. The silence was only momentary because, above them, someone started screaming, followed by loud voices shouting at each other.

Candy, Nikole, Michelle, and Tanya looked at the ceiling above them. Jennifer stared at the black stain that was spreading on its own across the front of Nikole's shirt.

"Nikole," Jennifer shrieked with the unmistakable sound of fear in her voice. "What is that on your shirt?"

Nikole looked down and pulled the front of her shirt out a little with both hands so she could see what Jennifer was referencing. The spot where the tendril had struck her was black. In the basement's lowlights, it appeared that the black mark was spreading. Before Nikole could get a good look at what it was, the lights shut off, plunging the women into total darkness.

The noise above them grew louder. The women feared that at any moment the floor above them would collapse and bring the entire bar area and patrons down on their heads. The building shook for a full five minutes then it stopped. The loud crashes and thuds above them stopped soon after. The silence was only momentary because above them someone started screaming. Followed by loud voices shouting at each other.

Chapter 7: 2022 - A Tempest Has Arrived

Main Street, which cut through the center of downtown Plano was utterly devoid of life. People had either gone indoors in anticipation of the coming storm or had already arrived at the three bars and one pizza place lining Main Street, deciding to stay there until after the storm passed. Animals that seemed more intelligent than people when approaching storms had fled and sought out safety away from the area. The storm that was not supposed to bring anything other than heavy rainfall changed to a full-blown tempest.

Heavy wind, accompanied by hail and a near torrential downpour, bullied and tormented the buildings and vehicles. Storefront windows shook, doors rattled. While the storm had the potential to be destructive, every building on Main Street escaped unscathed.

Except for The 4/26.

The roof collapsed, crashing down into the second floor, an easily avoidable situation if Zayan did not allow the building to deteriorate. This destruction by the storm caused a chain reaction, sending large support beams and debris down to the second floor straight through to the first floor. While it looked pretty horrible on the outside, it was a nightmare for the people inside.

Paco was still unsure of what was happening as the building started to shake. He had just come out of the bathroom and walked into the main bar area, where he found nearly everyone standing around. Paco heard screaming from the basement and suddenly, an adrenaline rush gave him a bit more focus.

As soon as Paco heard the loud crashing sounds coming from above, fear overtook him. He quickly rushed toward the door. His fingertips had just brushed against the door handle when a support beam came crashing through the ceiling, violently landing on top of him. The beam slammed into his head and shoulders and the force of the impact drove Paco into the floor. His skull was crushed, killing the old man instantly and the chain reaction broke just about every bone in his body. Bits of brain matter, bone and blood splattered out from under the beam. As the beam settled on top of Paco's carcass, it effectively blocked the door, sealing off the front entrance.

Still disoriented from Kevin's death and hearing her daughter screaming, April now had to witness the support beam crush Paco. As she winced, April turned her head just as her son, Christian, made his way over to her.

"Mom, get your head down!" he screamed as more loud crashes from more areas of the ceiling started to collapse.

Jeremy and Drew, who were still behind the bar, pulled Barb to the ground and pushed themselves as far under the bar area as they could go. Becka and Mikey, who were now hugging each other, quickly ducked, finding safety underneath a nearby table, soon joined by Sara and Lucy. Jason, Kyle, Kory, and Danny hit the ground where they were, placed their hands over their heads, and hoped for the best.

Billy grabbed Dustin yelling, "Dude, get down! He's dead!" pointing toward Kevin's body. "And you're gonna be, too, if you don't get your ass under a table or something." Breaking Dustin's paralysis, he and Billy dived under a nearby table already occupied by Eric and Hope.

Stacie turned around to look for Ernie. When she saw he wasn't there, she ran into the women's bathroom, leaned up against the door, and hoped for the best. Cris pushed Laura underneath an available table and covered her with his body. Zach, George, Paul, and Brett were all cramped underneath a row of tables lining the wall near the arcade golf machine. As soon as he was bunkered down, Brett looked around to assess the room. That is when Brett noticed Lori run for the smoking area's door.

Lori started running toward the back door that led to the smoking area. As she reached the door, a relatively large section of the ceiling had collapsed above her. Billy watched helplessly as his girlfriend was about to be obliterated by debris, ceiling tiles, and huge chunks of broken wooden beams. He never heard Lori scream, she never had a chance to. He reached out to her and began to call out, "Lori, look out!" but it was too late.

One of the beams had ripped apart leaving an extremely jagged edge behind. As though fate had stepped in and decided to have some fun; the pointed end of the beam forced itself through the top of Lori's skull, piercing her brain and killing her instantly. The rest of the now destroyed building materials continued pushing the beam further and further into Lori's body. The jagged edge of the beam was driven through her body at an odd angle. It had begun at the top of her head but ended up exiting her torso, effectively ripping her open, spilling organs and blood all over the floor. The beam was then pushed into her left thigh and finally came to rest in her right foot. Her body completely disappeared from view after being covered by a small mountain of debris. Billy stood by, frozen with fear and in complete shock.

And just like that door leading outside to the smoking area was now effectively blocked.

Holly, A.J, Deanne, Mark, and Sherri, did not move. They stayed huddled together near the pool table, still praying. Their prayers now transformed from those of Kevin's death to their own safety.

The building vibrated as more debris rained down onto the first floor. A third loud crashing sound bellowed as another support beam crashed through the ceiling. It plummeted into the fourth dartboard, collapsing in front of the second entrance door while piercing the floor. It leaned against the wall preventing that door from being opened.

That beam was the last of the significant destruction. Anything more that fell was tiny shards of tile, dirt, or dust. The wind outside was still ferocious, however, still vibrating the walls. It seemed the worst was over.

The room became eerily quiet. Everyone began to get off the floor or climb out from under their sheltered areas. Billy bolted for the mound of debris in front of the smoking area door. He began to dig into it with his bare hands, shouting Lori's name over and over. Brett, the only one who had seen what happened to Lori, ran towards the pile and began helping Billy.

Clearly confused as she stood up, April shouted out, "Is everyone alright?"

Brett, still digging, looked over his shoulder hollered, "No! Lori is buried under this shit!"

Jeremy and Drew ran from behind the bar to help Billy and Brett. Dustin crawled out from under the table and reached into his pocket, pulling out his cell phone. He turned it on and dialed 911. Dustin frowned as he put his phone to his ear. "Hey, I'm not getting a signal; can anyone else?"

Becka and Mikey crawled out from under their table. Carefully, they made their way over to their purses, which sat on an oddly undisturbed table. Shaking, each one pulled out their own phones, trying 911 as well. They looked at each other with wide, fearful eyes when they heard nothing from their phones as well. Wiping a tear from her eyes before turning to Dustin, Becka frowned, "I don't have a signal, and I don't think Mikey does either."

Suddenly, Stacie burst from the bathroom shouting, "Oh my God, Ernie is still outside!"

Jason stood up, dusted himself off, responding, "Holy shit! So is Robby."

Robby and Ernie were fixing to walk into the bar when the wind suddenly picked up. They heard splintering wood. Ernie looked above him, seeing a roof piece from the smoking area lift and fly off.

"What the fuck?" He said out loud.

Robby happened to be looking in the other direction. He saw what appeared to be a piece of sheet metal that had pulled free from one of the neighboring buildings as it flew towards them. Quickly, Robby shoved Ernie to the ground. They wound up crashing through one of the smoking areas' weak plywood walls onto the gravel below, just a foot from Robby's car. Ernie was about to protest, but from where he lay, he saw the large piece of sheet metal slam into the back door, slicing into it deeply.

"Shit, get in my car!" Robby yelled out. "We should be okay there!"

The men scurried to their feet and were luckily able to safely get into Robby's car. Rain and hail pelted the windshield, obscuring the men's vision slightly. They could still see enough to know that the roof had just collapsed into the second floor. Wayward bricks fell off the side of the building as portions of the walls started to shake and crumble. A brick slammed into Robby's windshield, cracking it into a perfect cobweb of broken safety glass.

"You got your phone?" Ernie asked, a bit out of breath. "We should call for help."

"I left it inside." Robby sighed, shaking his head with a frown.

"Me too." Ernie frowned.

"Fucking A," Robby blurted out, "That's convenient."

Inside the bar, people were coughing but started to regain their composure. Cris noticed a fine blackish mist in the air. "What the fuck is this shit we're breathing in April?"

April, who had started noticing it as well, coughed loudly, "Probably a bunch of dust and shit from upstairs."

Some people pulled their shirts up around their mouths and nose as others began to pull masks from pockets and purses. April didn't require face masks in her bar, but people typically had one on them now that it is in the second year of the pandemic.

April looked towards the front door and saw that with the way the support beam had fallen, going out that door was not an option. She looked past Christian and saw that the door leading to the smoking area was also blocked with a mound of debris that Billy, Brett, Jeremy, and Drew were digging through. Billy was still calling out Lori's name.

Cris noticed that the other two doors were blocked. He turned to look at the door by the first dartboard. Cris saw that the door was blocked by an extensive support beam. It had crushed the dartboard. He was the first one to say it, "Holy Fuck, April! " as he shouted across the bar, "We're fucking trapped in here."

"Are you shitting me?" April snapped back.

Holly, Deanne, Mark, Sherri, And A.J. stopped praying and began to separate from each other. Each one wandered aimlessly over to a table where they sat down. Holly was soon joined by Dustin, who had started crying.

Holly looked over at where Kevin's lifeless body lay and began to ask, "Is he...?"

Dustin sobbed louder as he shook his head "yes," pulling Holly in to hug her.

"Hey, heh," Kyle said with as cheerful a tone as he could. He stood up and dusted off his pants, "At least the lights are still on." Kyle instantly regretted saying something because as soon as those words came out of his mouth, the lights did indeed blink off. Thankfully, they were not in the dark long because April had battery-powered emergency lights installed in several areas around the bar. They, luckily, were in perfect working order. It took less than five seconds for each emergency light to turn on. Kory slapped Kyle in the back of the head, "Don't say another fucking word, you damn jynx."

Just then, more screaming erupted from the basement. April turned towards the basement door, "Holy shit! I never installed emergency lights down there."

Nikole, Jennifer, Tanya, Candy, and Michelle stood in the center of the dance floor as the lights went out. They were plunged into darkness. Candy screamed first, and soon all five women followed suit.

Nikole was the first to get her screaming under control. "Stop screaming, guys; that's not helping."

"What are we gonna do?" Jennifer asked.

Nikole stood up straight and said, "We slowly walk toward a wall and feel our way out. Everyone takes someone by the hand. Hopefully, we can find our purses or something."

Candy, who had been unusually silent, said, "Wait, I got my phone in my pocket." She fumbled in her back pocket briefly before pulling her phone free from her jeans. She turned it on and was able to get the flashlight on her phone to work. The light was bright enough that the women could see where the tables were. Slowly and still holding hands, the ladies walked over to the tables, but they realized their purses were missing as they got closer.

"What the fuck?" Tanya said out loud, "Where the fuck are our purses?"

Suddenly, a long black tendril, thinner yet similar to the one they saw earlier, slammed into Candy's phone, knocking it from her hand. Candy screamed and jumped back as her phone was slapped across the room.

Nikole jumped back as well and, still holding tightly to Candy's hand, screamed, "What the fuck is going on?"

Chapter 8: 1980-1984 - Lessons in Beer and Fear

Zeus was not aware that he was a secret or that Patricia was his mother. He did not know that he was purposely being hidden from the world to protect a wealthy man's reputation. If Zeus had known, he would not have felt so guilty about not sharing the secret of the mold and fungi he kept under his bed. Zeus learned rather quickly, however, that keeping secrets was relatively easy.

It turned out to be easy to grow mold and mushrooms. Zeus just needed some form of a moist environment. He always used a discarded article of clothing, one he may have outgrown. Adding water, Zeus made the clothing mildly damp. It was essential to provide the proper food. He would take his vegetables off his dinner plates and place them under his bed. While they decomposed, his friends, as he now referred to them, took care of the rest.

Soon, he had a nice size colony underneath his bed. By the time he was eight, Zeus had learned that not only did he have the ability to communicate with mold and fungus, but with just a little effort, he could control it as well. This discovery happened entirely by accident.

Although he was as close to normal of a child as Zeus could be, having only two digits on each hand often caused him to drop several components of whatever he made. Dropping items were commonplace while building a tower with wooden tinker toys and building blocks. Zeus would have to stop his simple construction and hurry to gather up the fallen piece more often than not. But on this particular day, something strange and wonderful happened.

Zeus watched as the little wooden dowel that he was about to use to help support his structure rolled away from him and underneath his bed. He let out a little sigh and said softly, "Too bad you guys couldn't get that for me."

To his surprise, five thin tendrils from what was now his black mold pet suddenly appeared from under his bed. Around the wooden dowel, each tendril curled. Zeus watched as the tendrils slowly made their way over to him, almost as if they were flowing through water, before placing the dowel in his outstretched hand. Zeus gazed as the dowel dropped into his waiting palm. He looked at the tendrils as they hovered slightly by him for a moment before quickly retreating under his bed.

"Thanks," he said with apparent childlike glee in his voice.

"You are welcome," came from under his bed in a voice that Zeus knew he could only hear.

It wasn't long before Zeus started using the mold (which was more readily available to him than fungus) to do his bidding. He found that he could send mold tendrils from under his bed throughout his room on minor fetch quests if he concentrated enough. He discovered that the task had to be reasonably simple. The mold could send out little tendrils of itself that grew thinner the farther it reached out, but it could never unanchor itself from where it had set down root. Zeus would need to move the towel or whatever article of clothing the mold was growing on to extend the reach. That all changed when he discovered a perfect growth environment for mold, the walls inside his home; mold had infested them everywhere.

Zeus made this discovery one day as he was taking a bath. He was lying down, allowing the water to rise just up to his cheekbones, when he heard whispers coming from the walls.

"He's the one who hears us," something whispered.

"He sees us as friends," came another.

Zeus sat straight up, saying excitedly, "Yes! I can; hello. Did you guys find a way out of my room?"

"No," replied another voice. "We are different. We are all over; we have watched."

Zeus smiled from ear to ear. He had new friends; he could hardly contain his excitement. He asked rather loudly, "Do you guys wanna be my friends?" just to be sure.

"Yes," said all the voices in unison. It took about a week to master, but before long, he was sending tendrils through the house to steal little things for him: cookies, chips, and other snack foods that Patricia felt needed to be regulated. During a run for a bag of cheese puffs, he discovered that he could see what his tendrils of mold were seeing with proper concentration. Soon, he explored the walls, taking in things most people would have never seen. When he was nine, Zeus had free reign in his home and investigated the newly opened bar below. This first exploration gave him an authentic taste of freedom.

Zeus was always careful, ensuring that the tendrils remained unnoticed when sent downstairs. Due to the dark interior of the bar, staying unseen turned out to be a reasonably simple task. The people that patronized the bar & grill always kept to themselves. They never really seemed to pay attention to anything around them. Instead, the people focused on whatever they were drinking, the game they were playing, or the friends they accompanied. Zeus observed as the more they drank, the happier they became, piquing Zeus's curiosity.

One Friday night, a night he was typically allowed to stay up late to watch his VHS tapes, Zeus sent a tendril down to fetch one of the beverage bottles that the people at the bar would drink. Zeus waited until after Patricia went to bed and the bar closed. Once it was empty, he sent a tendril through the bar and straight to a small cooler that sat behind the bar. With minimal effort, the tendril coiled around the bottle, playing a handoff game with other tendrils before finally getting the bottle into Zeus's hands.

Zeus turned the cool bottle in his hands. The glass of the bottle was dark brown. While he was unsure what color the liquid was inside the bottle, he could see bubbles rise to the top, almost like soda. The label on the bottle was red and white and had a word on it that he was not entirely familiar with. Zeus did not care; he had seen several people downstairs drink these bottles. They always looked happy upon completion of the beverage. He was optimistic that whatever was in it had to be delicious.

He struggled with the bottlecap before figuring out that he needed to apply some leverage to one side of the cap before it popped off. Once opened, he took a sniff of the beverage inside and winced. It smelled like a mix of bathwater, and the bread Patricia would make. Maybe this bottle was spoiled, he thought. Zeus held the bottle to his nose once more, sniffed, and considered that perhaps it was not quite so bad. Zeus decided that the beverage was safe to drink after the third and final sniff, and he brought the bottle to his lips and took a big swallow.

The beverage was disgusting. Zeus found himself immediately gagging and regretting his decision. He tried his best to swallow what he had left in his mouth but wound up spitting a majority of what he hadn't consumed all over his bedroom floor. Zeus held the bottle away from him, making a beeline toward the bathroom. He quickly dumped the remainder of the bottle's contents into the sink and, in another moment of poor decision making, tried to bury the bottle in the small trash can Patricia kept by the toilet. Zeus covered the bottle with some used tissues and empty toilet paper rolls. Feeling somewhat safe, he made his way back to bed. Zeus had already started to feel a little light-headed as he quickly drifted to sleep.

Patricia woke the following morning unaware of what Zeus had done the night prior. She went about her mundane minor cleaning tasks and got ready to prepare breakfast. Patricia noticed the trash can next to the toilet being full and decided to empty it. It had a little weight as she lifted it off the ground. She shrugged it off and took the can into the kitchen to dump the trash into the larger garbage can. Patricia would have never noticed the beer bottle if it had not clanged off the side of the kitchen's larger metallic trash can. Puzzled, she looked down and frowned when she saw the dark amber bottle sticking out from underneath a couple of loose tissues. She knew immediately from where the bottle came. She didn't drink and knew there was no beer in the house, which could only mean one thing. Zeus somehow snuck out of the house and into the bar below using his superior intellect. She wasn't extremely angry or disappointed. Patricia was scared. Zeus was a child, after all, and children are curious creatures by nature. What scared Patricia was that Zeus could have been seen, and staying unseen mattered most.

Gripping the bottle in her hand, Patricia took a deep breath and marched toward his room. At this moment, she needed to be firm. The boy's survival was in her hands, and right now, he needed discipline. She put on her angriest face and marched right into his room. Zeus was still asleep. Patricia considered waiting until he woke but decided this had to happen now. She needed him to know the seriousness of what he had done.

"Zeus, wake up now, young man!" Patricia demanded in a loud, angry tone.

Zeus fluttered his eyes open. When he saw what Patricia held in her left hand, his eyes went wide with fear, sitting straight up. "Mama, I, uhhhhh, I," He stammered, but Patricia cut him off.

"You could have been seen, boy," she said, practically yelling. "What the hell were you thinking?"

Zeus contemplated telling and showing Patricia what he could do with the mold for a brief moment. He paused as he knew she would either not understand or, he thought, could even drop dead out of fright. Zeus decided to keep this a secret. "I was careful; no one was there."

Patricia, clearly frustrated, pounded on her right hip with a balled-up fist. "I do not care!" She growled. "You are a special boy, but there are assholes out there." Patricia waved her hand around her, not meaning just the people around them directly but the world in general. "Those people," she continued, "will hurt you."

Zeus's heart began to beat fearfully in his chest. He was always apprehensive of the outside world. He never knew how much Patricia never wanted him to venture out into it until now.

"They will kill you," she explained. "Those people will call you a freak; they will beat you." Patricia sighed and held up her hand, showing it to Zeus. "Just look at your hand, baby, and you will know you are different." Shaking her head, "Those bastards out there in the world want nothing to do with things that are different. They fight each other over opinions, beliefs, and skin tone."

Zeus noticed that she had started to cry. He opened his mouth to apologize, but she waved him off. "I understand, I do. But right now, the world is not ready for you. They will be scared; they are fearful. Worse yet, they are mindless creatures when confronting their fears. Instead of attempting to understand you, they would rather kill you. Be afraid of the world. Be mindful. Be smart."

Patricia held up the empty bottle while Zeus looked away in shame. "Well, how was it?" she scoffed.

"Gross!" Zeus frowned while sticking out his tongue. "I poured it down the sink."

Patricia nodded her head. She almost asked him how he had gotten out, but she knew it did not matter. Patricia was well aware that Zeus was a genius for his age. The only hope she had was to make him understand how the outside world would treat him. She didn't want to make him scared; she needed him to be scared.

"Okay," she said happily with his answer. "What I want you to do is think about what you have done. Never leave this house again. I can only protect you here. If you get away from me, I can't save you if they get a hold of you."

Patricia walked over to Zeus and gave him a deep hug. "Mama loves you, okay, baby? But more than that, know I will keep you safe."

"Thank you, Mama," Zeus replied as he snuggled into her.

Patricia broke the embrace, "Okay, get dressed and let's have breakfast."

Zeus let Patricia go, watching as she walked away. He felt fear, but he also felt sadness and anger. Why would the people outside hurt him? What was wrong with him? Zeus looked down at his hands and realized just what Mama was trying to help him understand. He decided to stop thinking about it. He swung his feet out of bed and began to change out of his pajamas. Zeus had just put on a fresh T-shirt when a voice rose from behind his walls.

"We will protect you!" it hissed.

Zeus looked up at the wall, "Really?"

"Yes," said the voice. "We will protect you. You do not need to be afraid. They should be afraid of you."

"But Mama said....." Zeus started to reply.

"Yes, she did. But Mama will not always be here. We are forever," the mold stated in a cold flat tone. "Let us show you who should be terrified."

Zeus nodded, "Okay, but only if Mama can't find out."

Before hissing, the mold was silent, "Good; tonight, we will show you how weak they are." Not knowing who "they" were, Zeus nodded and left his room to enjoy his day.

The day progressed like any typical Saturday; he ate good food, watched cartoons, and played a few games with Patricia. Before he knew it, the sun was setting, and the moon was high in the sky. After watching a movie with Patricia involving a boy and his dragon, she declared it was bedtime. Patricia tucked Zeus in for the night before going to bed herself. The mold patiently waited until Patricia was fully asleep before disturbing Zeus, who had forgotten all about their discussion earlier.

"Are you ready to see fear?" the mold inquired.

Zeus sat up straight in his bed. Before he could protest, he saw the bar's interior once more. A tendril of mold traveled close to a wall, unseen by everyone in the bar at that present time. The tendril made its way towards the men's restroom and slipped unnoticed under the door. Standing at a urinal was a man who was relieving himself. The man seemed rather happy, whistling as he urinated. Zeus watched from the perspective of the mold as it curled itself around the man's left ankle. The tendrils jerked violently before the man could respond, causing the man to slip and fall backward, screaming.

The mold swiftly retreated under the door and pressed itself against the wall. Zeus watched a couple of men run towards the bathroom to investigate the man screaming inside.

"Dave, you alright?" one man asked.

"Dude, what the hell is going on?" asked another.

Before they could open the door, Dave came bursting through the door, struggling to pull his pants up. He was still slipping and sliding, and he looked scared. "Something fucking grabbed me, man," Dave said out of breath. "It tried to pull me down."

Both of the men laughed, "Dave, you've been drinking awhile."

Dave, who managed to get his pants on, stood up, "No, no fuck that! Something grabbed me. Nah, something was in that bathroom."

The men continued laughing. Dave, now frustrated, growled back, "Fuck you guys." He turned and stormed out of the bar.

Zeus watched as Dave left. The tendril of mold, then, quickly retreated, disappearing back into the wall where it had come, returning Zeus's vision to his room.

"You see," said the mold, "they, too, can be scared."

Zeus nodded his head but did not speak. What he saw terrified him. It was not that Zeus had just witnessed the mold he befriended scare some random guy. Zeus was more frightened at how indifferent and horrible Dave's friends had just acted. Of course, no one saw the mold. No one watched the man called Dave fall. These friends of Dave's didn't even care. A couple of months before turning ten, Zeus witnessed what he learned about being afraid. Seeing those guys have no care for their friend Dave, Zeus realized Patricia was right. People were terrible. He knew they would genuinely destroy him if they treated a normal-looking person with such indifference. Thank goodness he had Patricia and the Mold.

Chapter 9: 2022 - Division Begins

A black haze still floated in the air. It was not as thick as the dust once was but still noticeable if one was inclined to look for it. April felt anxious and on the verge of a total panic attack. She looked around. Her newly renovated bar was destroyed. Three of her regular patrons lay dead, while everyone else was probably breathing in something toxic from whatever Zayan had going on upstairs. To top it all off, they were trapped.

"What the fuck are we gonna do?" Lucy questioned out loud as tears streamed down her face. Christian walked over, put his arm around her, and did his best to console her.

"That's a good question," Jeremy said. He had stopped digging through the rubble, making his way to the other side of the bar. He decided to help himself to a beer.

April closed her eyes and took a deep breath, or as deep of one as her little cloth mask would allow. "I don't know." was her only answer.

Meanwhile, Dustin had walked over to Kevin's body. Dustin was thinking about how he even got into this situation. He only agreed to play in this dart league as a favor for Cris and Laura. Kevin, who needed a team, was then given one, with Dustin and Holly added. At first, Dustin found Kevin's antics bizarre. Dustin did grow to like the guy. Kevin's humor and energy were infectious. Seeing Kevin's corpse tore Dustin's heart out as he realized the jokes had officially stopped.

Kevin's body was face down; he had fallen against the dartboard and had crumpled a little to the left of the machine. There was no blood, and if he hadn't watched Kevin's electric dance of death, one could say Kevin was lying there playing possum. Dustin knelt beside

Kevin, "Sorry, Buddy." As Dustin stared at Kevin's body, a small amount of anger began to bubble up inside. This anger began to focus on April.

Dustin thought April should have known better. She had to have known this would have happened sooner or later. Sure, Dustin knew her pathetic excuse about no one being allowed in the apartments upstairs. But, after the first time the roof leaked, April should have closed down the bar. She should have forced the landlord to repair the damage or refund her money. Dustin was becoming angrier. His thoughts continued to meditate on the potential of what April should have done. There were plenty of other vacant buildings she could have opened a bar. But no! She stubbornly had to have this one. Now because of that stubbornness, people were dead. Dustin looked over, seeing that Billy and Drew were still digging in the giant mound of debris that still trapped Billy's girlfriend, Lori. Dustin shook his head. He couldn't begin to imagine the pain Billy was going through. He then looked back at Kevin's lifeless body. Dustin noticed the gun sticking out of the back of Kevin's pants.

Dustin knew Kevin was a fan of guns. He knew Kevin had a conceal and carry permit. Dustin did not realize that Kevin had a firearm on his person at the bar. He did not care, at this point, why Kevin had a gun. Dustin pulled Kevin's .45 free from the holster and placed it in the front pocket of his oversized baggy sweatshirt. Dustin looked around and made sure no one noticed what he had done before smoothing Kevin's shirt back down. Dustin discreetly stood up. He wasn't going to even tell Holly about the gun he had hidden in his sweatshirt. For some reason, Dustin just knew that he would need it. He looked over at Billy once more before heading over to the table Holly was sitting at, but his sister Laura started to scream just before he did.

Laura was still under the table with Cris as she watched Dustin stand up from leaning over Kevin's body. Cris had asked Laura to stay put and to leave her mask on. With her acute condition, Cris did not want her health to worsen. Laura was starting to feel claustrophobic. She pulled her facemask down to breathe unrestricted. After a couple of deep panicked breaths, she began to notice her vision was starting to darken. Soon, all lights and colors faded. She was thrust into total darkness, even though she had her eyes open. Her state of panic intensified; unable to control herself, she started to scream.

Cris knew about April's knowledge that the roof caving in was a possibility. He was beyond frustrated, ready to have a showdown with April, when Laura suddenly screamed hysterically. Cris turned where he had left his wife and saw that Dustin, his brother-in-law, was already trying to help Laura out from under the table. Cris completely changed direction, sprinting over to his wife.

"What's wrong, baby," Cris implored as he helped Dustin pull Laura out from under the table.

"I can't see!" Laura screeched. "I can't fucking see."

Cris and Dustin helped Laura to her feet. Dustin moved out of Cris's way. Dustin found his way back over to Holly. She was standing up, watching the commotion with Deanne and Mark.

"What's wrong?" Deanne asked.

Dustin shook his head and then evilly glared over toward April. "Laura can't see; she just went blind."

"What?" Mark gasped. "How is that possible?"

"Who the fuck knows," Dustin continued. "Probably all this black shit hovering in the air. Or that toxic dust that came down with the roof."

Cris ignored the conversation happening behind him. Instead, Cris focused on his wife. He took her head in his hands and said, "Baby, I'm here."

Laura reached out widely with her hands. She stopped panicking when her fingers brushed her husband's scruffy face. "I can't see," she cried. "Baby, everything just went black." Cris noticed that his wife was facing him, but her eyes were not locking on him; it was almost as if she was looking past him. Cris took her by the hand and led her over to Holly and Deanne.

April had begun to walk over to the basement door when Cris adamantly made his way to her. April could still hear the women screaming; she knew they were trapped downstairs in total darkness, and she needed to help them. April nearly had a hand on the doorknob when Cris called out her name.

Meanwhile, Becka, who had taken her mask off after the dust had settled, talked to Mikey. Becka paused as her mouth formed the shape of the letter O. She saw something that looked like a rather sizable iridescent caterpillar crawling across the bar. "Holy shit, do you see that?" Becka asked while pointing to a spot on the bar.

Mikey looked to where Becka was pointing and sneered, "Uh, there's nothing there."

Becka, feeling more confused than ever, looked up at Mikey. Becka's eyes widened. Mikey's face looked as if it was inflating and deflating in random areas. First, Mikey's left eye swelled and then settled back to normal. Next, her right cheek followed the same pattern. As Mikey opened her mouth, another caterpillar fell out of Mikey's mouth, landing on the bar.

Becka jumped back with fearful eyes and looked up at Mikey. "What is going on with you?" She gasped.

Mikey was now clearly confused because nothing was going on with her. Unbeknownst to Mikey, Becka was seeing something that Mikey could not. "What are you talking about?" Mikey questioned as she reached out toward Becka. At that very moment, Cris began to scream at April.

"APRIL!" Cris screamed as he walked over to April in a threatening manner.

April stopped in her tracks. In response, Billy and Drew stopped digging in the debris. They walked over to see about the commotion. Drew turned and noticed something very odd happening between

Mikey and Becka. He decided to see what that was about, leaving Billy by himself.

"What, Cris?" April responded.

"You just had to have your fucking moment, didn't you?" the anger rising in Cris's voice. "Now, look around you. We're fucking trapped in here; Kevin's dead, Lori's dead, and my wife cannot see!"

April took a step back. She held her hands up defensively, "Cris, calm down. We're all upset; let's just relax."

"Fuck you!" Cris snapped back. "You knew something like this could happen." Cris did not know where this rage was coming from, but it was here. Maybe it was the stress bubbling over. Perhaps it was all the pain he had endured. It could even be the fear of the potential of losing his wife. Whatever it was, right now, he was beyond angry. Someone was going to pay the price. That, someone, was April because this was her bar, and she knew it wasn't safe. She had to! "You fucking knew it wasn't safe," Cris snapped.

April stared at Cris in utter disbelief. If she knew the roof had any chance of collapsing, she would not have opened the bar. Zayan assured her the building was safe. Cris, understandably angry, was just lashing out like a child. April would be no one's whipping post.

"Fuck off!" April shouted back. "You know better than that; I had no idea this could happen. But yes, I feel like shit about this. Kevin and Lori were both my friends, too, Cris." April took a deep breath. "Look, go by your wife and calm the fuck down. I need to check on my daughter." April took a step back toward the basement door when Dustin pulled out Kevin's gun.

"No, fuck you bitch!" Dustin exclaimed as he pointed the gun at April. "This is your fucking fault!"

Everyone went silent as Dustin took a step toward April. Kyle and Kory jumped to their feet and began to walk toward April with the apparent intent to help. Dustin turned slightly, pointing the gun at the guys. Dustin screamed toward them, "Sit the fuck back down now!"

"Dude, calm down," Christian pleaded as he put his hands up, taking a step toward his mother.

"Fuck you," Dustin snapped as fresh spittle flew off his lips. "Your fucking mother opened this goddamn deathtrap, knowing full well what could happen. She is not going anywhere until help shows up."

"Hey, don't talk to my son like that!" April snapped back, being the defensive mother she is.

"Fuck your son," Cris jumped in, saying, "Dustin's right."

April's eyes widened. Were they really blaming her? She lowered her head as tears began to well up in his eyes.

Cris looked to his left, saw the ax Joel had left behind and walked over to pick it up. Everyone, still in shock and frozen in place, just watched silently as he did so—everyone except for Becka, who pulled on Drew's shirt sleeve to ask him a very peculiar question.

"Do you see the llama?" She asked with a confused smile on her face.

Drew turned to look at her. He loved Becka more than anything. He knew that she could be a bit quirky at times, but this was indeed odd. The question was so bizarre that he just looked at her for a moment. Drew tilted his head, "Whhhaaat?" he breathily asked. Before Becka could answer, Holly stood up and began to yell at Dustin.

"What the fuck are you doing, you idiot? Dustin, what the fuck is wrong with you?"

Dustin turned his head and watched as Holly walked over to them and placed herself between the gun in Dustin's hand and where April stood. "You fucking know better!" Holly lectured. "Look, everyone is upset about Kevin, but that is not her fault!"

Just then, Cris walked over with the ax in his hands, "Shut up and sit down, Holly; stay out of this!"

Holly, totally undeterred, turned to Cris, "Or what? You'll chop my head off?" Mocking him, Holly scoffed, "Oooh, a big man needs an ax to threaten a woman. You limp dick bastard!" Both Cris and Dustin staggered as if Holly had slapped them. Holly was always the quiet type, but she was being very vocal right now.

Still sitting at the table, Laura shouted out, "My husband does not have a limp dick, Holly!"

"Thanks, babe!" Cris called back.

"Really?" Holly snapped back, clearly frustrated. "This dumbass is waving an ax around, and you're worried about a dick shaming." Holly lowered her head and shook it. "What the fuck is wrong with you morons?" She turned her attention back to Dustin and held out her hand. "Give me the gun, Dustin."

Dustin looked over at Cris, who was shaking his head, 'no'. Holly stood her ground and growled, "Now, Dustin!" Dustin looked at Holly and tears welled up in his eyes.

Slowly he placed the gun in Holly's hand and tremblingly said, "You're right, I'm sorry."

Holly took the gun. Instead of lowering it safely, she spun it in her hand. Holly wrapped her hand around the handle, placed her finger on the trigger, and pointed it at Dustin's head. "I know," she chuckled sarcastically before pulling the trigger.

Dustin's head exploded in a crimson shower of blood, bone and brain matter. In seconds, Holly's face was covered in bits of Dustin. Christian got a great deal of Dustin all over him too, as he was standing beside Holly when she fired the gun. Dustin's body stood still for a moment before wavering slightly and ultimately collapsing to the ground.

"What the fuck, Holly!" Jason shouted from the back as he shielded Sara from the sight of Dustin's corpse.

Laura shouted out from her spot under the table, "What the hell just happened?"

Cris walked over to his wife, still holding the ax. "Holly just fucking blew Dustin's head off." Cris put an arm around Laura to console the grief he knew she would feel over her brother's death.

Holly turned her head, saying to April, "Go check on your daughter." Unfortunately, no one saw that Billy was making his way slowly over toward Holly.

Ernie and Robby heard the gunshot as they were still outside, staring at the remains of the smoking deck. They knew that door was now blocked. Each man looked at the other and ran to the front of the building.

"Was that a gunshot?" Robby asked as he trailed slightly behind Ernie.

Ernie did not answer. Instead, he started calling out for Stacie. When the men arrived at the main front door, they pushed on it. They realized it, too, was blocked. Ernie tried to bang on the door, but the amount of collected debris seemed to muffle his pounding. Robby ran over to the second door in the front and shouted, "This one is blocked, too."

"What the fuck? I need to get in there." Ernie demanded.

Robby took a deep breath, "Ok, let's calm down. I am sure help is on its way." The violent wind had subsided, but the rain was still coming down pretty hard. He looked around and saw that while the streets were empty, a couple of the other buildings around them had shining lights. "Look. Let's run down to one of these bars and call for help," Robby suggested. He turned and saw that Ernie was not there. Instead, the door that led to the apartments above the bar was wide open.

Robby ran over to the door and looked up the dark staircase that led upwards. He could hear Ernie's footsteps on the stairs.

"Dude, what the fuck are you doing?" Robby hollered up the stairs.

"The floor caved in. Meaning there are holes in the ceiling. I can get down into the bar," Ernie hurriedly explained.

"Dude," Robby sighed in a disgusted tone, "that's a fucking bad idea." Against his better judgment, Robby stepped through the door and bolted up the stairs to catch up to Ernie.

Chapter 10: 2022 - Something on the Dance Floor

When Nikole heard the gunshot ring out above them, she jumped. The bang spawned a chain reaction causing each girl to jump almost like they were doing the wave.

"What the hell was that?" shaking, Candy looked at the other ladies.

"Hell if I know," Tanya shook her head and let out a quick laughing sigh, more out of nerves than anything.

Nikole stared up at the ceiling, with her head cocked to one side, while squinting her face with confusion. Someone had just fired a gun inside her mother's bar. She had no idea what was going on. Nikole did know she did not want to stay in the basement with that snake. Nikole's eyesight was starting to adapt to the darkness. She began to see the outlines of the bodies of the other women. When she could see the shapes of the chairs and tables, Nikole figured that if she could lead the women towards the stairwell. They should easily be able to find their way upstairs. Before she had a chance to lead the way, a voice hissed up at her. The sound came as if whoever was speaking was on the ground.

"Stay with us," the voice beseeched.

Nikole tilted her head and, out loud to no one in particular, asked in an overly prominent confused high-pitched voice, "What did you say?"

Candy needed to explain, "I asked what that sound was."

"I said something, but I can't remember," Tanya said, with a shiver in her voice.

"I didn't say anything," Jennifer shrugged.

"Me either," Michelle stammered, "I just want to get the fuck out of this basement."

Puzzled, Nikole looked down and, at first, saw nothing but darkness. A faint blue glow began to emanate from the front of her shirt. "It was ussss," the voice hissed again.

Nikole's eyes widened. Her mouth opened as if in slow motion, and she reacted how anyone would have in that situation.

She screamed. Not just loud and scared, but a blood curdling, ear piercing, "AAAAAAAAAAHHHHHHHHH!"

While screaming at the top of her lungs, Nikole beat at the front of her shirt. Slowly, a bit of rationale began to creep into her mind. Hitting the shirt while she was wearing it was only hurting herself. Nikole decided her best course of action was to pull her shirt off over her head. She was wearing a sports bra and a tank top underneath, but even if she weren't, she still would have torn that shirt off. Fear outranked modesty at this point. In seconds she had her shirt off over her head before throwing it across the room.

It did not appear that Michelle thought the situation was as dire as everyone else was thinking. "Nikole, what the hell?" Michelle shouted out as she reached for Nikole. "Calm down, girl."

Nikole couldn't calm down, though. She just kept screaming hysterically. Candy felt the need to take charge of the situation. She spun the hysterically screaming woman around as she stood next to Nikole. Hoping for the best, Candy swung her open hand towards what she was hoping would be Nikole's face. She was on target; the quick and crisp slap echoed throughout the basement, silencing Nikole.

"What the fuck?" "Who slapped me?" Nikole shouted as she was no longer screaming.

"I did," Candy answered rather sternly." And if you scream one more time like that, I'll do it again," adding in a head bob and finger swag. Candy then reached her hand up to caress Nikole's now burning cheek. "I'm sorry. I needed you to stop screaming. Now, what was that all about? Girl, what happened?"

Nikole took in a deep breath, "That shit on the front of my shirt started...." She paused, knowing what was about to come out of her mouth would sound insane. "... talking to me."

"That's bullshit, girl. Maybe April needs to add some ventilation down here. You going crazy." Jennifer asked.

"You guys know that thing we saw in the closet?" Nikole tried defending herself. "It slapped me on my chest. It left behind like a residue or a stain." She lowered her voice to almost a whisper, "It was...talking."

Tanya was doing her best to listen and understand what Nikole said, but nothing coming out of her mouth made sense. Tanya planned on saying that, but she stopped. Something coiled around her left leg. Tanya looked down, straining her eyes, trying to see what was there, but it was still a little too dark. Suddenly, a faint blue glow appeared from out of nowhere. Tanya noticed that this blue light not only wrapped around her foot but also trailed away from her. She tried pulling her leg back, but whatever had coiled around her violently jerked backward. Whatever had her tightened its grip. Tanya felt immense pain radiate up her leg, finding herself in the grips of panic. Tanya started to scream before anyone could respond to Nikole.

The other four girls jumped in the direction of Tanya, trying to see what was wrong. They could somewhat make out her silhouette, which appeared to be flailing. Tanya violently was pulled backward. Her feet pulled out from underneath her. She fell back, her head smacking onto the hardwood that made up the dance floor before quickly bouncing off, effectively silencing her scream. She felt her ears pop loudly as her head began to feel light. As the women stared harder, trying to comprehend what they saw, Tanya's figure seemed to be floating and moving away from them. Indeed, Tanya found herself jerked towards the maintenance room. Not that she knew where she was going, but only that she was moving.

Then Tanya was gone.

What no one could see was that the impact Tanya's skull made on the floor had caused it to split at the back and as she was being pulled across the room, leaving a thin trail of blood behind her.

"Tanya!" Nikole shouted out, "Where are you, babe!"

Candy called out, "Tanya! Girl, where'd ya' go?"

Tanya did not answer; she could not answer. All she wanted to do was sleep as she vaguely noticed being pulled across the floor. When the giant black tentacle coiled around her foot stopped pulling Tanya across the room, she had passed out. No one in the basement knew that Tanya's unconscious body was lifted into the air, feet first. When her head was about six feet off the ground, that thing coiled around her leg, let her go. It quickly retreated into the maintenance room. Tanya's body fell a total of six feet back to the floor. When her already weakened skull collided with the hardwood, it shattered, sending a sharp fragment of bone into Tanya's brain, killing her instantly.

Nikole, Candy, Jennifer, and Michelle never saw any of it happen. They heard a lot of commotion and rustling. The most distinct sound the ladies did hear was Tanya's body as it crashed back to the ground. It was a loud wet smack and, then, silence.

"Tanya?" Michelle whispered.

A ray of light suddenly appeared over where the stairwell was. The ladies heard a man and a woman arguing at the top of the stairs. It was of no matter to them. All four women turned toward the stairwell as their hearts leaped for joy. The door opened meant they could get out of the basement. All four women locked arms after Tanya's abrupt abduction slowly made their way over to the stairs. At that moment, the two people at the top of the stairs stopped fighting.

Along came a sudden scream, followed by the unmistakable sound of a person tumbling down the stairs.

Chapter 11: 2022 - A Bloody Hat Trick

Billy was a short man in stature. Most of the time, he could maneuver unnoticed. Tonight it was paying off as Billy made his way over to Holly, holding out his right hand. All he needed was for Holly to let her guard down, and he knew he could easily take the gun from her.

No one was paying attention to Billy. Everyone was staring at Dustin's corpse. Zach was the first one to tear his eyes away from the scene in front of him. He began to walk over to the bar's main entrance, followed by George and Paul. Zach was on the verge of a panic attack, and he found the only thing that kept him calm was hard work. Zach figured he would try his best to clear the doorway. George and Paul were shell-shocked. Unable to think clearly, they were going along and doing whatever Zach was doing. Soon, Kory, Kyle, and Danny joined the trio.

As the six men went to work on the front door, Brett and A.J. went back to work to try and clear the rubble off of Lori's body.

Becka still thought she saw the llama, as her mind barely registered the gunshot. Mikey walked in front of Becka and began to snap her fingers. "Hey! Girl. Talk to me. Are you there?"

"Shhhh," Becka whispered, holding her fingers up to her lips. "You'll scare it."

Drew turned his head away from the grisly scene before them. He turned towards Becka, concerned, "Hey, you good?"

Becka turned only her head towards Drew, smiling, "Fine, babe, why do you ask?"

Drew snickered a bit, "Because you just asked me not five minutes ago if I saw a llama. Now you're telling Mikey she'll scare it." His face turning more serious and concerned, Drew looked into his wife's eyes." Did you hit your head?" he inquired as he leaned in closer.

Becka smiled and turned away from Mikey and Drew. She took a step forward with her hand out as if she was trying to pet something.

Barb and Sherri took cover behind the bar when Holly fired the gun. They had acquired a bottle of vodka and were content to hide behind the bar and drink their troubles away.

Stacie started panicking because she knew Ernie was outside. Her mind kept showing images of her soon-to-be husband crushed underneath the remains of what once was the smoking deck. "Oh my God," she shrieked. "I need to get out of here. I need to check on my Ernie!"

Hope and Eric walked over to console Stacie. As Hope focused on Stacie, Eric never took his eyes off Cris, still holding the ax. Eric watched as Jermey walked over and stood next to Cris.

Christian walked away from the carnage and walked into the kitchen area, followed by Lucy. They were then joined by Jason and Sara. Lucy watched as Christian started digging around underneath the small prep station. "Babe, what are you doing?" She asked.

"Looking for a fucking rag," he answered. "I need to get that asshole's blood off my face."

Jason, who just stepped into the tiny kitchen, corrected him, "Dude, that's kind of harsh."

"Fuck that!" Christian exclaimed. "That asshole pointed a gun at my mom."

"Still, he didn't deserve to be shot like that," Jason responded.

"Hey, that's on, Holly," Christian shrugged as he defended his perspective. He then stood up with two rags wiping Dustin's blood off his face. Christian knew he was not going to feel clean for a while, but right now, he just needed to get as much off as he could. Lucy stepped up to him, took the other rag, and began wiping the other side of Christian's face. That was when a loud shouting match between April and Cris erupted from the bar area. Christian, hearing the distress in his mom's voice, looked down. On top of the prep station, a large butcher's knife rested on the butcher's block. Taking the knife by its handle, Christian stepped out of the kitchen and began to walk over to his mom.

"Mooovvveee Cris," April sternly demanded. Cris was now standing in front of the door leading into the basement.

"Are you fucking kidding me?" Cris loudly snapped back at her. "Holly just killed Dustin, and you're yelling at ME?"

April looked down at Dustin's body and was surprised by just how indifferent she felt about what had happened. April considered herself a good person. She stood by her faith and would even throw people out of her bar for taking the Lord's name in vain. But, for some reason, the sight of one of her regular dart players' corpses had little to no effect on her.

April looked up, shrugging, and in an icy response, "Oh well! Now move so I can check on my daughter."

Cris reluctantly stepped aside. April walked over and opened the door to the basement. Before she could descend down the stairs, Billy realized that everyone, including Holly, was distracted. He decided to go for the gun.

Holly did not see or notice Billy until it was too late. She honestly didn't think anyone would try to go against her after what she had just done, so Holly had started to relax a little. Before she knew it, Billy had wrapped his hand around the top of the gun and had pulled it free from her hand. He then held the weapon in both hands and pointed it at Holly.

"Don't fucking move!" Billy shouted, "Just no one fucking do a thing!"

April stopped in her tracks and turned around. "Are you fucking kidding me, Billy?"

"Cris is right.," Billy exclaimed. "You knew this could happen, yet you went along and opened up anyway. Now my Lori..." He paused and teared up, turning towards the rubble Brett and A.J. were standing beside. They stopped digging, watching what was going on. "... She's gone," he continued.

Cris started to chuckle in a sarcastically evil tone. "Okay, April, why don't you step away from the door and go stand by Holly until we figure out what to do with you."

It was at that moment that Deanne had had enough. "Oh my God!" she yelled out. "What the fuck is wrong with all you idiots?" She got up, shaking off Mark's hand as he tried to hold her back.

"Honey, no," Mark pleaded.

Deanne, though, was not listening. She was pissed. "Look. You two blame whoever you want, but that does not mean those girls need to be trapped in the basement." She pushed her way past April and Cris. Deanne turned and pointed her finger in Cris's face. "You know what, asshole? If you thought this bar was such a death trap, you didn't have to keep coming back."

Cris's eyes widened. "Me? The asshole?" He sneered with evident shock in his voice. "My wife is fucking blind because whatever this shit is that is floating in the air." Cris turned to April, shouting, "All because this bitch had to have her fucking moment."

By now, everyone had stopped what they were doing. They all focused on the disturbance by the basement door.

Still holding the butcher's knife, Christian stepped towards Cris, "Shut the fuck up, Cris. No one talks to my mother that way."

"What are you going to do, you damn Asian-lookin' chihuahua?" Cris said with a laugh. "Lucy, come get your fucking bitch before I split his head in half."

"Oh fuck you, Cris." Deanne roared. "You limp dick piece of shit. You know you wouldn't be so tough if you didn't have that ax." Deanne gestured towards Billy, "Or if your little bitch here didn't have Kevin's gun." She shook her head, "You're both fucking jokes, and to be honest, you're just whiney little pussies." Deanne chuckled, "Now I'm going into the basement. Try to stop me."

What happened next caught everyone off guard. Still holding the ax, Cris shoved the handle in Deanne's direction. He knocked her in the chest, causing her to lose her balance. As Deanne tried to turn and catch herself, she felt her already weakened ankle snap once again. She was in free fall and tumbled backward down the stairs.

The left side of Deanne's head connected with the third step from the top. The impact was so violent that her cheekbone and eye socket collapsed as she was rendered unconscious. Her body, now limp, began to tumble loudly and clumsily down the stairs. The fourth step was a bit uneven and when she got there, the impact flipped her around somewhat. On the fifth step, her arm had gotten caught under the weight of her body and broke, causing the bones to protrude through her skin. The resulting exposed bone splinter, acted as a knife and punctured her chest through her ribs as she continued to the sixth step. Her head connected again on the seventh step. Between the weight of her body and the momentum of her fall, Deanne's neck had snapped. Upon reaching the eighth step, Deanne's heart stopped. At the ninth step, her leg was sliced open by the exposed bones from her broken arm. Blood trickled down the stairs as she fell, making everything a bit more slick. Deanne's body skipped right past the last three steps and her lifeless body made a nauseating wet slap when it finally reached the basement floor.

April watched her friend fall. April shrieked, "Deanne!" as she bolted down the stairs after her friend. When April reached the bottom of the stairs, she saw the blood flowing from Deanne's nose and ears.

Deanne's eyes were lifeless. April glared up the stairs at Cris and watched as he gave her a sick sinister smile.

Mark did not quite know what had happened at first. Once it registered in his mind that Cris had just pushed Deanne down the stairs, he jumped out of his seat and attempted to run towards Cris. Before Mark could make much of a forward movement, he was tripped and quickly restrained by Jeremy.

Cris looked down at April, "You stay down there with your friend. I'll get us out of here." He violently slammed the door closed.

"Mom!" Christian shouted as he started to rush forward.

Cris turned towards Christian. Holding the ax up, Cris warned him as he shook his head side to side. Lucy knew full well what that meant. She put her hand on Christian's shoulder and pulled him back. "Stop, babe; he'll kill you." Christian hesitated but backed up beside Lucy.

"Good boy!" Cris said sarcastically before walking over to an empty table. He quickly pushed it in front of the basement door, effectively blocking it from opening until the table could move.

Jeremy had Mark in what looked like a rather painful chokehold. As Mark began to cry, Jeremy dragged him over to Cris. He slammed Mark to the ground at Cris's feet and stepped back.

Mark got to his knees and looked up at Cris, "I'm going to fucking kill you," as spit and snot dripped from his face.

"I don't doubt that," Cris scoffed, bringing the ax up over his head. "So I might as well get you before you get me. You understand."

Then without warning, Cris brought the ax's blade down into the center of Mark's forehead. There was a loud wet thunk noise and then there was a bit of resistance as Cris tried to wrench the ax free. He placed a foot on Mark's chest and pulled back as hard as he could, freeing the ax from Mark's skull. For a moment, blood trailed in an arch from the fatal wound in Mark's head. Droplets of blood splattered from the ax painting the nearby wall as Mark's dead body slumped over.

Everyone in the bar recoiled and began to scream. (Except for Becka. She was still walking towards the corner by the arcade golf machine with her hand out.) Cris raised the ax high above his head, dripping Mark's blood onto his upper half, and shouted, "Everybody. Shut the fuck up!"

People began to grow silent as they backed away from what was going on. They attempted to retreat to the farther corners of the bar, except for a few. Still in their positions near Cris was Billy, who still had the gun pointed at Holly, and Holly, who had her head up and glared at Cris. Jeremy stood behind Cris with his arms folded across his chest.

"Lemme see the gun Billy," Cris demanded as he handed the bloody ax to Jeremy. Billy gave the gun to Cris and stepped back. Still smiling his sick sinister smile, Cris looked at Holly and called out.

"Babe!" He shouted, "I got control of the bar,"

Laura let out her loud "Woot Woot" call before asking, "What are we doing now?"

"Well, I am going to get us the fuck out of here," Cris answered. "But first, what do you want me to do with Holly?"

Laura was silent for a moment as her thoughts swirled in her head. Dustin could be an asshole, but he didn't deserve to die. The answer was clear; she knew what needed to be done. "Kill the bitch," Laura called back rather coldly. Cris looked at Holly, shrugged, and without saying a word, pulled the trigger.

The gun fired. The bullet ripped through Holly's chest and obliterated her heart. The shot left an exit wound the size of a softball in Holly's back as the shell sank itself into the corner of the bar. There was still enough velocity in the bullet that if anyone had been standing behind Holly, it would have killed them as well. Holly's eyes went wide as the bullet tore through her. Her eyes then rolled back into her head; she was dead before her body collapsed to the floor.

Cris smiled, "Okay, that's that." He handed the gun to Billy, commanding, "If anyone steps out of line, blow their fucking heads off."

Cris turned toward Jeremy and gestured for the ax. Jeremy willingly gave up the ax. Cris turned and walked over towards Zack, George, Paul, Kory, Kyle, and Danny. They had all stopped digging in the debris by the front door to watch what had transpired. "Don't stop, boys," Cris ordered as he placed the ax on his shoulder. "Keep fucking digging." Cris turned around and shouted towards A.J. and Brett. "You two keep trying to dig out Lori for Billy." He paused to look at Becka, who was now standing by the arcade golf machine. She was acting like she was petting something. Shrugging while he rolled his eyes, Cris turned around and faced everyone else who was in the bar.

As the men went back to work, Cris scanned the room. All eyes were on him. He stood up a bit straighter. He knew right then and there that he was firmly in control.

Chapter 12: 1985-1991 - Spores and the Mess They Make

Just a few months shy of his eleventh birthday, Zeus had grown quite skilled at sending the mold out to explore and gather forbidden snacks for him on his way to becoming a preteen. He considered the mold a friend. It wasn't until after his eleventh birthday that he discovered that the mold was not the only thing he could talk to or that it was just an extension of himself.

Keeping a wet towel under his bed for his mold to grow before entering the walls to live yielded a strange and welcoming result. Small yellow fungal caps or odd-looking mushrooms had sprouted from the mold beds. Zeus did not think anything about it; he figured it was something else to learn about and look after. It wasn't until he was investigating the feathery underside of one of the caps did he discover that mushrooms were just as chatty as mold.

One day as Zeus pulled his towel, now covered in mold and yellow mushroom caps, he heard the mushrooms let out a faint hiss as he pulled the towel into the light.

"Hurts," they hissed.

Zeus widened his eyes and slowly pushed the towel back under his bed. "I'm sorry," he whispered apologetically.

Zeus laid down on his stomach and stared at the towel. He squinted his eyes slightly to obtain a better look at his new friends. It was hard to see them, that was until the mushrooms themselves began to cast a low blue glow. He pulled his head back and let out a loud surprised gasp. Zeus quickly looked towards his door and waited for the inevitable cry of Patricia calling out to check on him. He heard her footsteps make their way from the kitchen. He scrambled and grabbed a nearby comic book, sat straight up, and began to feign interest in what he was reading. There was a brief rap on his door. His door slowly opened as Patricia stuck in her head. "You okay, child?" She asked.

"Yes, mom!" Zeus replied as he held up his comic book. "I just got to an exciting part of the book, and it caught me off guard, is all."

Patricia smiled; her heart warmed whenever he called her mom. "Okay, dear, dinner is almost ready. Why don't you wash up and join me." She looked at him, and he could see the slight frown on her lips. "You have been spending a lot of time in your room." After a slight pause, she continued, "Maybe we can play a game tonight or watch a movie?"

That nice man Zayan had just brought them a new VCR along with a considerably large stack of VHS tapes; also, she was right. He had been spending way too much time in his room with the mold. Plus, the cover art on the box of one of the tapes looked interesting. It had a young man holding up what appeared to be a sword made of light in front of a sinister-looking giant black mask. It had the word Star and the word Wars in the title. Whatever it was, it had to be cool. Besides, the mold went throughout the house so he wouldn't feel too bad. They could somewhat join him in the other room. The mushrooms, though, were firmly rooted to the towel.

"Sure thing, mom!" A smile beamed across her face. She blew him a kiss before leaving, closing the door behind her. As he heard her footsteps retreat down the hall, he stuck his head back under his bed and saw that the mushroom caps still had a blue glow around them. "That is so cool," Zeus said in amazement.

"We only need a little light to see," The mushrooms sang in unison.

Zeus had grown quite comfortable with hearing a chorus of voices in his head. The mold's voice was always the same, masculine and deep. The mushrooms were a welcomed change as they were more feminine and light, giving him an easy way to distinguish who was talking to him. He had so many questions he wanted to ask, but they would have to wait. He needed to spend time with his mother.

Patricia smiled when she saw Zeus walk into the kitchen. "Hey dear, dinner is not quite ready. But you can go into the living room and pick out a movie to watch." Zeus smiled and slowly made his way over to the stack of VHS tapes. When he returned to the kitchen with his pick, Patricia was not surprised to see that he picked out a movie critics called a once-in-a-lifetime science fiction masterpiece. Patricia stared lovingly down at Zeus's smiling face as he held up the tape. Her heart skipped a beat. She really had grown to love this boy. Whatever he wanted, she was going to make sure he had. Patricia stared at the tape in his hands, "That's fine, dear; go set it on the T.V., and I'll get the chicken out of the oven." Zeus smiled back, skipped into the living room, and did as asked. Then he sat down on the couch and waited for dinner to finish cooking.

The night went very well. Dinner, as always, was delicious. The movie itself was indeed a spectacle. Zeus was on the edge of his seat the entire time. He was overjoyed when he found out there was a sequel and that they had it on tape. The movie made such an impact that Zeus made little laser noises as he skipped back to his room at night's end. As he opened the door to his room, he went to turn on his light. That was when he saw glowing blue flecks floating around his room.

"What?" He questioned confusedly aloud, not expecting an answer.

Suddenly, a chorus of feminine voices spoke up with an explanation. "This is how I multiply," the voices sang. "People call it spores." There was a pause before they continued. "Careful to not breathe us in. You can get sick."

"Uhhh, you're all over my room!" Zeus exclaimed, holding his arms up. "How do I not breathe you in?"

"They cannot hurt you," came a more masculine chorus of voices. Zeus knew that was from the mold. "We have spores as well. It can hurt others, but you are safe."

"We are friends," the feminine voices declared.

"As are we?" questioned the mold.

"We can all be friends," Zeus chimed in, a little overzealous, unable to contain his excitement.

There was a completely childlike unified cheer when all the voices blurted out a resounding "Yay!" making Zeus smile.

Zeus began to familiarize himself with how spores work in the following weeks. The science behind it was not complicated, and he was beyond happy to learn using the new group of books the man called Zayan was leaving behind. By the time his twelfth birthday arrived, Zeus still did not find it strange that this man would drop off whatever toys or books he requested. The man's motives were still a mystery, and Zeus's curiosity was indeed starting to be piqued.

Zeus decided it was time to ask Patricia who the man was. The conversation upset Patricia and caused her to speak condescendingly to Zeus. "You do not need to know him," she asserted. "You only need to know that he serves us, and that is it; don't ever come to me with such a stupid question again!"

Shocked and a little upset by what she had said, Zeus decided it was best not to argue. Instead, he made his way back to his room where his friends were.

"That was mean," said the soothing voices belonging to the mushrooms.

"She's just protecting me," Zeus responded with an unmistakable hint of doubt in his own words. "Besides, I shouldn't really care where all these things come from," he reasoned out loud.

'We can get you whatever you want," came the deep voices belonging to the mold.

"I am sure you guys could if you could leave the house," Zeus clarified. "But like me, you're stuck here. At least you guys can go downstairs," he finished with a sigh. Zeus had started to grow quite jealous of others being able to come and go with leisure. Deep down, he knew it was for the best. The interactions he saw in the bar below through the eyes of mold made him nervous about meeting anyone else. Why Patricia chose to stay, though, was a mystery to him. One that he did not need to know the answer to. Little did Zeus realize that he would have pretty much answers to all the questions in his head in a couple of years.

Life going from preteen to teenager was pretty much the same physically and mentally for Zeus as for every other child, with the exception he had to do it away from the world. He doled out his angst and rebellion to only one person instead of a few. Patricia knew this was coming and had prepared herself for it. She often had Zayan bring her a few bottles of wine as she coped with Zeus's behavior. Strangely enough, his growing pains were not as bad as she had feared. Unbeknownst to her, Zeus was up to some very unwise inappropriate behavior, and technically, he did have many "friends" to help him sort it out.

After reading more into the effects that fungal and black mold spores could have on the human mind, he made the amusing discovery that the spores could cause people to see things that were not there. Or, as the book put it, hallucinate. He had discovered that just like the mold, the spores produced by his now overgrowing garden of mushrooms, as well as the black mold that inhabited the walls and dark spaces under the furniture in his room, could travel freely. Being a confused puberty-ridden teen with hair growing where there once was none, Zeus acted out by sending spores into the bar area below. Those actions caused a slight bar brawl. Zeus being fifteen and full of unspent testosterone, found the incident hilarious.

Since that evening five years ago when he was just a ten-year-old kid, this was the first time he had allowed the mold to travel downstairs, letting him see things through their vantage point. He had discovered a year earlier he could see what the spores were seeing, allowing for numerous vantage points. He had typically used his friends to steal snacks and beverages from the kitchen when Patricia was asleep or busy. Tonight Zeus needed a bit of chaos. The spores traveled from his bedroom window and gently floated down to a slightly cracked window into the bar below. Tendrils of mold had already snaked their ways through the wall and were now low to the ground pressed up against the baseboard of the walls, low enough that no one was able to see them. Zeus knew that spores had to go where the wind took them. For reasons entirely unbeknownst to him, tonight, the spores in his room reacted differently. He reveled in this because it suited his nefarious purposes.

There were only about six men and the bartender in the bar at the time. That was all Zeus needed for his little practical joke to work. To him, that was all this was. Entertainment. A joke. In all actuality, what happened that night could have been a lot worse.

The spores quickly entered the men's bodies via their nasal cavities and opened mouths. With each breath the men took, the spores rapidly traveled through them. Mike, who also happened to be running for Mayor of Plano, was the first to feel out of sorts.

"Guys?" Mike asked. "Does anyone else feel a little out of sorts?"

Jamal, a town alderman and friend of Mike, answered, "Yeah, now that you mention it, I am feeling a little dizzy." Jamal held up his half-empty glass of whiskey and called out, "Hey Tony, what's in this brown water you served me?"

Tony, the bartender, was at the far end of the bar talking to two men who worked next door at the pet food store, Keith and David. Tony looked up, "Just your usual brother," then his eyes went wide. Tony was unsure what he was seeing, but it looked as if both Jamal's and

Mike's faces were melting off. Tony closed his eyes tightly and shook his head. When he opened them and looked back, both men's faces had returned to normal. At that very moment, two men named Austin and Blake, sitting at a table near the bar door, began to argue.

"Did you just call me a bitch?" Austin snarled.

Blake looked at Austin, ready to say something, but instead busted out laughing. Austin had what looked to be a small army of colorful crickets running across his face. There, of course, were no crickets but a hallucination caused by the number of spores both men had inhaled.

Blake did not know why the crickets made him laugh instead of showing some sign of concern, but he could not help it. His laughter naturally angered Austin, who heard voices in his head questioning his manhood. Austinl stood up and punched Blake in the face. Blake fell out of his chair, but instead of fighting back, he just kept on laughing.

Tony stood straight up, hollering over at them, "Okay, asshole, that's it; you're outta here."

Austin did not hear Tony. All he could register was the sound of Blake's laughing, which just infuriated him. Austin walked over and slammed his foot down on the side of Blake's skull. This violence prompted the four other men to jump out of their chairs and rush Austin. The guys all felt a little woozy as they moved. David even stumbled, nearly falling, but still, they managed to restrain Austin from doing any actual harm to Blake. Granted, Blake would not have noticed because he sat up, continuing his fit of laughter.

"Dude, you alright," Jamal asked as he let go of Austin. He was confident that the other three men had a secure grip on the man and approached Blake. Blake looked up at Jamal and immediately started laughing louder. Jamal had a small army of bright purple ants marching in and out of his open mouth. Blake did not know that what he saw wasn't real, nor why he found the disturbing scene so hilarious. All he knew was that laughing felt good.

Upstairs, Zeus was also laughing. He knew how and what the man was hallucinating because he precisely guided the spores to show each man. Zeus was on the floor with his nature book opened to a page about insects. He requested the mold to infect Blake's mind with the random images. Meanwhile, Zeus was softly repeating the few curse words he knew over and over in Daryl's head, causing the man's anger to grow. Zeus still had surprises in store for the others. One joke, though, caused things to go a little too far.

Tony had started to walk around the bar to successfully end whatever confrontation was going on when he saw what looked to be a rather sizable snake on the ground. Not many people knew this, but Tony was deathly afraid of snakes. The sight of one just randomly slithering across the bar floor set Tony into a complete panic. He let out an echoing scream and ran towards the door. Tony ran past the five non-laughing men, screaming. Instead of opening the door like an average person, he crashed right through it. The sound of breaking glass and splintering wood was loud and worrisome.

Jamal jumped up from where he was and ran to the now-destroyed door. Mike and Keith let go of Daryl and ran to join Jamal. What they saw was truly disturbing. Tony was now writhing on the sidewalk screaming about a snake, with blood freely flowing from several different wounds on his body. At that moment, there was the sound of a scuffle behind them. The three men turned and saw David and Austinl were amid a very serious fistfight.

Jamal stood tall and, at the top of his lungs, screamed out, "What the fuck is going on?"

Mike turned to answer Jamal. When he saw that Jamal's face had been replaced with one of a cat, he just burst out laughing.

The police and an ambulance arrived less than five minutes later. With no serious injuries, the hallucination appeared to be a matter of possibly a mild form of alcohol poisoning. No one ever suspected the true culprits.

Zeus, though, could not contain himself. He was laughing so hard that it stirred Patricia awake. She called down the hallway in a thunderous and stern tone, "Zeus go to bed now!!!" His laughs became a snicker, but he decided that he had enough fun and quickly called his friends back home.

Rumors traveled like wildfire in Plano. The incident at the bar was quickly all anyone could talk about, something that Zeus took great pride in. This event inspired him to send his mold and fungal spores out to cause more mischief, none leading to significant fights like the first time. A part of him did feel guilty that two men did suffer injuries, even if they were in hilarious ways. The spores mainly caused people to hallucinate things based on the items in his room, often to hilarious results. Mostly harmless, of course, but the hallucinations never resulted in anything as horrible as his first mischievous deed. Zeus was puzzled as to why the spores never chose the hallucinations. In the late summer of 1991, a stunning revelation was revealed to him.

"Because the decisions are yours," the chorus of voices answered him.

He was shocked. Even though he was only four feet tall and nearly an adult, Zeus, now sixteen, fully understood the statement. "You mean...." he began to ask. Before he could finish his questioning, the voices spoke up.

"Yes." The voices stated. "We have consciousness; we have mobility. But you tell us what to do."

Zeus sat on the edge of the bed. Everything made sense now. He understood why he was the only one to see the mold, hear the mold, and interact with the spores and the mushrooms. On that fateful day, it was all suddenly clear. Patricia, his mother, did always say he was special. He realized now just how right she was. Zeus not only befriended the mold but controlled it. For the first time, he felt freedom unlike any other he had ever felt.

Zeus knew just how much control he actually had. From that moment, everything changed.

Chapter 13: 2022 - Basement Tragedy

April stared daggers at Cris as he yelled down at her. She jumped to her feet and bolted up the stairs as she watched him slam the door. The sound of the slamming door echoed loudly in the narrow stairwell. April tried to push against it when she arrived at the door, but it did not budge. She heard screams and yells come from inside the bar. Her bar! Something horrible was happening on the other side of that door. At that very moment, she felt helpless. Out of the blue came another gunshot. Everyone that was screaming fell silent. April began to back slowly down the stairs as she heard Nikole's voice rise from the bottom of the stairs.

"Who's there?" Nikole called out.

April could detect the fear in her daughter's voice. "It's me, baby," she yelled back as she slowly made her way back down the stairwell.

The darkness was thick in the basement. April instantly regretted not putting in emergency lighting downstairs. She quickly shooed that thought away as that was the last thing she needed on her mind at the moment. Right now upstairs, Cris had lost his mind. Worse yet, he was armed.

April reached out the moment she made it to the bottom of the stairs. She instantly found Nikole. After Nikole let out a loud, "MOM!" both women embraced.

"What's going on up there?" Candy interrupted the reunion.

"It's Cris; he lost his fucking mind and just killed Deanne!" April answered in one single breath.

Jennifer let out a loud gasp, "Where's Deanne?"

April paused in silence and tried to peer into the darkness towards what she thought was the bottom of the stairs. She looked down with a frown and then back up again with a sigh. "She's down here with us," April said, trying to choke back tears. "Cris pushed her down the stairs."

"Are you sure she's dead?" Michelle asked, not believing anyone could be dead.

April nodded before realizing how ridiculous that was in the darkness and said, "Yeah, I saw the body, the blood; it wasn't pretty."

Nikole, who still held tight to her mother, let out a little sob, "Well, it's no better down here; something killed Tanya."

A chill ran up April's spine. Nikole had just said something, not someone. She thought her word choice was not literal, so April clarified, "Who killed Tanya?" Concern and fear sounded heavy in her voice.

"Not who, mom," Nikole corrected, "What."

April froze, clearly shocked by Nikole's response. Her daughter undoubtedly felt that something, not someone, killed Tanya. April was absolutely mind-blown. She had a psychopath running loose upstairs, and now according to her daughter, something menacing was on the loose down here. For whatever reason, April found herself surprisingly calm. Given everything that had just happened, she was not anxious at all. Maybe it was her adrenaline, or perhaps it was just her mind blocking things out; whatever the case, she just felt relaxed, ready to fight but relaxed all the same.

"Well, whatever," April shrugged with a small laugh. "We need to find the tables," April commanded before asking, "Where are your phones?"

"No idea," Candy answered first. "I had mine, but the same thing that killed Tanya knocked mine out of my hand, and it's somewhere down there."

"And it stole our purses!" Jennifer chimed in.

April began to pat her pockets. She was pleasantly relieved when she felt her lighter, an old school flip top zippo, was in her front pocket. She fished out the lighter and flicked it to light with ease. April was not much of a smoker, but a good bar owner always has a light available for their smoking customers.

The glow of the small flame was enough to light up the area around them. April raised her hand into the air casting the glow farther. At that moment, every hair on April's body stood on end. She saw the outline of Tanya's body not ten feet away. "Son of a bitch!" April hissed through her teeth.

The sight of Tanya's body brought fresh tears to Nikole's eyes. "Mom, what the fuck is going on?" She implored.

April did not respond but, instead, walked over to Tanya's body. Blood was pooling around the young woman's head. April immediately looked away. April noticed Nikole's shirt on the ground, where she turned away to look. "Nikki, why did you take your shirt off?"

"Don't touch it!" Nikole demanded in her high-pitched squeal. "There's some black shit on it. I think it is part of what killed Tanya." Nikole paused for a moment, batting her eyes, holding back years. "I think it's alive because it talked to me."

April shook her head, rolled her eyes, and mumbled to herself, "Seriously?" before walking over to the shirt. Still holding the lighter in one hand, she bent down and picked it up. There was indeed a black residue on the front of the shirt. As she brought the lighter close to whatever was on the shirt, she watched as whatever was there suddenly recoiled in multiple directions. This movement left a space free of residue near where the heat of the lighter was. April pulled her hand back, at first, out of fear. She began moving the Zippo again to an area where the black residue was. Once again, whatever was on the shirt retreated from the heat. It moved with an almost oily-like speed to another section of the shirt.

"Whatever this is," April called out as she dropped the shirt and stood up, "It hates the lighter."

Before anyone could answer, Michelle started screaming.

Michelle stayed behind everyone. Her eyes had grown accustomed to the darkness, and she could see everyone else's silhouette in the weak light cast by April's lighter. Michelle was confident that her back was firmly against a wall, protected, able to see whatever was out there coming. Unfortunately, she did not see the slim tendril snake its way from the ceiling. Michelle didn't even feel its presence until it wrapped around her neck, lifting her off the ground. Before her feet left the floor, she began to scream.

April raised the lighter as high as she could and quickly made her way to the other girls. From the dim glow of her lighter, April saw that Michelle was about two feet off the ground. The heels of her feet were kicking against the wall.

Candy acted first. She raced over and grabbed Michelle's right foot and tried to pull her back down, though Candy felt her efforts might be in vain. Jennifer ran over and reached out for Michelle's left foot but couldn't reach it in time. Whatever coiled around Michelle's neck pulled her upwards with such force that Candy was lifted off the ground too. This frightened her enough to let go.

April cried out, "What the fuck?" She helplessly watched as Candy let go of Michelle's foot and landed abruptly on the floor. Now Michelle slid up the wall at inhuman speed. At this point, she had stopped screaming and was only making loud gurgling noises. The light from April's lighter was just bright enough that everyone could clearly see Michelle's ascent toward the ceiling.

Jennifer, Candy and April watched as Michelle's head connected violently with the wooden beams in the ceiling. Her head unnaturally contorted to the left, accompanied by a loud, nauseating snap. April heard that same sound earlier as she watched Deanne plummet down the stairs and recognized right away that Michelle was dead. Whatever was holding onto Michelle's body, suddenly let go.

Candy, who was still seated on the floor, stared upwards with fresh tears streaming down her cheeks. Michelle's body was a good ten feet off the ground when the unforeseen beast let her go. Candy, paralyzed by fear, resigned herself to her fate and simply laid down on her back. Instead of rolling out of the way, she put her hands out and started to scream. Michelle wasn't a heavy woman, but she wasn't skinny either. Her body had fallen in such a way that a majority of her body weight landed on Candy's head, slamming it violently against the floor. While not a fatal blow, it did knock Candy unconscious. Michelle's left knee struck Candy in the throat with such force that it ruptured her larynx, causing her to drown in her own blood.

"Candy! Michelle!" Jennifer yelled out as she ran frantically over to check on her now fallen friends. Nikole quickly grabbed Jennifer by the arm and pulled her back.

"No!" Nikole scolded. "Whatever got Michelle and could do that could easily still be there!"

"But, they could still be alive," Jennifer pleaded.

April made an annoyed sigh and pushed her way past the two women towards the prone bodies of the dead ladies on the ground. Michelle's corpse had managed to roll off of Candy. By the amount of blood that April saw flowing from Michelle's nose and ears, she knew for sure the woman was gone. April knelt and looked over at Candy. Her heart quickened when she noticed the blood flowing from Candy's mouth. April was hoping not another person was dead. "Candy!" April shouted as she aggressively shook Candy's unresponsive body. Knowing what had become of Candy, April stood up and made her way over to her daughter and Jennifer. "They're gone." Both women erupted in painful-sounding whines.

"What are we gonna do, Mom?" Nikole asked.

Instead of answering, April winced and switched the hands holding the lighter. She had gotten lost in her train of thought. Her thumb was too close to the lighter's flame, which caused her to burn herself slightly. She brought her thumb to her mouth, sucking momentarily, trying to alleviate the burning sensation. It dawned on her how the black stuff on Nikole's shirt had reacted to the lighter a moment ago. It wasn't responding to the light but the heat. As the light bulb went off inside her head, "Nikole, where are the tables?" she inquired.

"Where they always have been, Mom," Nikole replied, an air of confusion in her voice.

"I thought you guys said they were taken?" April, clearly growing a bit angry, asked rather loudly. April did not understand why, now, the rage was there.

"No, our purses were, "Jennifer chimed in, trying to diffuse the tension.

April nodded dismissively. Holding the lighter out in front of her, she stomped off towards where her basement tables were, with Nikole and Jennifer following close behind. April quickly arrived at the tables and handed the lighter to Nikole. April flipped over the table closest to her. She grabbed one of the legs of the table and, with a couple of hard kicks, was able to wrench it free. At that exact moment, they heard another gunshot ring out overhead, followed by loud stomping and sounds of a struggle.

"Gotta move fast," April hissed as she turned and grabbed another table leg and kicked it free. She repeated the steps, handing a leg to each girl. Without a word, she snatched her lighter from Nikole's hand.

"Mom, what's wrong?" Nikole questioned.

April did not have an answer. Gone was her calm feeling, replaced by a burning rage she had never felt before. April resisted the strong desire to slap her daughter across the face. Instead, she wordlessly held the lighter up higher until she saw what looked to be the familiar tie-dye scarf that Tanya always wore. It was lying on the floor just a few feet away from where the tables were. April stomped over, snatched it up, and began to wrap it around the head of the table leg rather tightly. April lifted the lighter to set the flame against the thin fabric. It caught fire rather quickly. April hoped it would not burn too fast as she pocketed her lighter. The glow that her makeshift torch cast had covered a larger area as she spotted Tanya's body.

"Girls, follow me," April commanded as she walked over to Tanya's corpse. She then looked at Nikole and Jennifer and ordered, "Take off her shirt."

"Why?" Nikole asked.

Before anyone saw it coming, April slapped Nikole in the face. "Just fucking do what I told you to." April had no idea what had come over her. She felt as if someone else had control of her. April shook the thought out of her head. She was desperate, angry, and afraid.

Nikole recoiled from her mother, raising her hand to her cheek. She did what her mother told her. With Jennifer's help, both women removed Tanya's top.

"Tear it in half.," April said. "Then you each take a piece and wrap it around the tip of your table legs."

Nikole and Jennifer realized April's plan and quickly went to work. When their makeshift torches were complete, April brought them to life by using the head of her torch. The combined light of the torches cast a wide, welcomed, and warming glow. Nikole looked around the bar and asked, "What now, Mom?"

April looked in her daughter's face and, in a very stern voice, replied, "We take back my fucking bar!" before storming off in the direction of the stairs.

Chapter 14: 2022- Nightmare Upstairs

"Dude!" Robby shouted as he bolted up the stairs after Ernie. "Slow the fuck down, will ya'!"

Ernie, though, did not slow down. He was hellbent to get back to Stacie, and at this point, Robby was just along for the ride. Ernie was familiar that no one was allowed in the upstairs apartments, but he was pretty sure the apartments had just collapsed into the bar area. As far as he was concerned, whatever rules April's landlord had given were pretty much moot at this point.

The apartments were pitch black. There was enough light shining through the windows that Ernie could see where he was going. He paused at the landing to get his bearings. That was when he caught the horrible stench that hung in the air. It was the smell of decay and mold. The odor was enough to gag Ernie, who quickly pulled his shirt up around his nose. He looked to his left, then his right, and was about to head down the hallway. He knew the direction of the bar, but before he proceeded, he felt a hand grab his shoulder. Ernie quickly raised his fist, ready to strike. He took a deep breath when he saw it was Robby. "Dude, I almost knocked you the fuck out," he stated.

Robby, with his hands up in defense, "Whatever, look, we should really leave."

Ernie shook his head, "You fucking leave. I'm going to find a way to Stacie." He turned and made his way down the hallway. Robby rolled his eyes, following Ernie. As soon as he arrived, the smell also hit Robby, but Robby had a strong stomach; it didn't bother him so much. He was walking close behind Ernie when he whispered, "What the fuck is that smell?"

Before Ernie could answer, another gunshot rang out below them. "Stacie!" Ernie called out in a loud whisper as he sped up down the hallway, Robby right on his heels. The hallway ran the length of the building into two open areas that once were a kitchen and a living room. The kitchen was on the left, and the living room was to the right. Robby looked around the living room while Ernie took the kitchen.

Robby was in the living room for less than a minute when he saw the hole in its floor. Light was filtering up through the hole. He also heard loud voices but dismissed them to nothing significant. He figured it was just people currently panicking due to being trapped after the recent storm. Robby noticed plenty of room for them to wiggle through the hole in the floor and safely land in the bar area below. Smiling to himself, he yelled towards the kitchen, "Ernie, you were right, dude, we can get down to the bar."

Robby heard Ernie yell back, "I fucking told you! I am on my way." Robby heard Ernie's footsteps start to approach. Without warning, Ernie cried out, "What the fuck; Robby get over here! Something's got me!"

Robby jumped up and ran to the kitchen area; what he saw chilled him to the bone. There was a room adjacent to the kitchen. The door of this room had rotted off its hinges, now lying in the kitchen. (Not shocking, considering the disrepair the building was in.) Legitimately heinous were two enormous black tentacle-looking things stretched out from the doorway. Robby stood there frozen for a moment. He saw the tentacles had wrapped around both of Ernies legs and were pulling him towards the opening.

Ernie was pounding furiously at the tentacle wrapped around his left leg. Creatively swearing, calling the strange thing every profane name in the book, "Let go, asshole motherfucking cocksucker!" Ernie blurted out.

Robby felt a misplaced fit of laughter rise in his chest. He quickly fought it off and scanned the ground near where he stood. Upon spotting a 2x4 board, he quickly seized it and ran over to Ernie. Robby began to beat the tentacle wrapped around the man's right leg. Either feeling pain or threat, the tentacles quickly uncoiled and retreated into the room.

"What the fuck was that?" Ernie yelled.

"I-I d-don't know," Robby stuttered.

Ernie looked down and found what looked to be a roughly three-foot length of steel pipe. He assumed it probably was a broken pipe that carried water through the walls at some point. Where it came from really didn't matter to Ernie right now. He felt the need to arm himself and immediately go on the defensive.

Light was filtering in through the windows casting shadows through what once was a kitchen and the unknown adjacent room. From where they were standing, they saw what looked like someone, about the height of a middle school child, run across the back of the room.

"Dude, someone's in there!" Robby said.

Ernie heard Robby's statement and agreed. Instead of responding to Robby, though, Ernie called into the darkroom, "Hey fucker; get your ass out here!"

No one came out, but instead, someone answered. "Just leave," came a low, scratchy voice, "I will spare you."

"What the fuck?" Robby said out loud, looking around, trying to find the voice owner.

Ernie was past the point of talking. He raised the pipe above his head. With a bellowing roar, he ran into the room.

"Dude, really?" Robby called after him. He gripped harder, his length of 2x4 tightly, and ran after Ernie. Robby had nearly collided with him because what Ernie saw caused him to stop his charge and stop dead in his tracks. Robby walked past Ernie and looked ahead. What he saw caused him to say to Ernie, "Dude, I told you it was a fucking mistake to come upstairs."

Standing with his back against the wall was a man of short stature. He wasn't actually standing on his own feet. He, at first glance, looked to be levitating. He had two lengths of tentacles lifting him off the ground. The light from the two windows in the room revealed that it was once a bedroom, with the remains of what appeared to be a mattress on one side confirming the fact. More black tentacles looked like they had sprouted from the man's back. They hovered, double the size of the man. The tentacles bent slightly to avoid contact with the ceiling. Ernie and Robby stared blankly at what stood in front of them.

"GET OUT!!" The man screamed at them. Ernie flinched back as two of the tentacles thrust themselves forward. Robby thought he was ready for an attack. He swung his 2x4 with such ferocity that he struck the first tentacle. It sailed aimlessly past them, hitting the wall on their left. Both men ducked the second one. They rushed towards the abomination, both holding their makeshift clubs high in the air.

Ernie swung his pipe towards the second tentacle, hoping to make room so he could either confront or make contact with the man standing before them. Robby, who had closed in, was nearly ready to make contact when the other two tentacles lowered and swung sideways, striking Robby in his abdomen. Before Robby knew what was going on, he was in a backward freefall to the right. Smacked with such force, he had let go of the 2x4, which sent him crashing through one of the windows.

Robby was now grasping for thin air as he fell the full two stories backward. Unfortunately, his head connected with the roof of his car, the back of his skull imploding. The rest of his body crashed into the ground. Robby was dead before his body even came to a complete stop.

Ernie did not see Robby hit the car, but he heard the sound of the man's head bouncing off of metal. Ernie raised the pipe slightly, like a softball player ready to smash a run out of the park, "You are going to pay for that, you motherfucker."

The man suddenly began to move to his left side towards what looked like an enormous hole in the wall. "That was your fault!" the man said. "You never should have come back in; this is my time now."

Ernie paused and lowered the pipe slightly, "What the fuck are talking about?"

Instead of answering, the man made his way towards the hole in the wall. "This is my time. I am leaving tonight!"

Puzzled, Ernie watched as the man disappeared into the dark hole, retreating further into the apartments. Deciding it was not a good idea to check on where the man went, Ernie turned on his heels, ran back down into the kitchen, and then made his way towards the living area where Robby had found the hole.

When he got to the hole, Ernie heard what sounded like a lot of shouting, followed by three more gunshots. Startled, he jumped back but went back to the hole. He saw Stacie walk into view. Ernie's heart leaped for joy, and he started to call out her name. "Stacie, baby, Stacie, I'm up here," he shouted.

Stacie looked up. Ernie could see she had her hand clasped tightly around her throat. She smiled weakly up at him before removing her hand. That was when Ernie noticed her hand covered in blood. A small river of blood flowed from a gaping wound in her neck. She took another step towards Ernie before collapsing on the floor.

Ernie let loose a guttural cry, "STACIE!" He sat down and began to kick away the loose boards trying to make the hole large enough for him to jump down through. His weight and the force of his kicks caused the floor around to shift before it collapsed, sending Ernie crashing feet first to the bar area below.

Chapter 15: -2022- A Llama's Bad Advice

As Cris surveyed the bar, he could tell people were upset with him. Christian and Lucy cast cold death stares in his direction. Hope would glance over and just bury her head back in Eric's chest while Eric sent a clear look of disgust in Cris's direction. Mikey was angry, and her death stare showed it. Drew looked confused, probably because his wife was over by the golf machine cooing at something, although he had no idea what she could be cooing at. Cris looked over at Jeremy and Billy and saw that they had been joined by Jason and Sara. Brett and A.J. were still digging, refusing to look over their shoulders. Stacie still had not moved from her spot in front of the bathroom door. Barb and Sherri were out of sight, but Cris could hear them sobbing from behind the bar. He took a deep breath and decided to address everyone; he didn't care whose side they were on.

"Ok, now that we got the stupid shit out of the way, we can get down to business," he began. "Look, you guys are ok with me. I have no problem with the lot of you. Just stay in your lane. Shut the fuck up, and I won't have to... well... handle any more problems." Cris thrust his thumb over his shoulder, referring to Jeremy and Billy, "Now, I am going to make sure that these guys get us out of here. Look, hate me, I don't give a fuck, but I will do whatever I can to make sure my wife is ok."

Laura let out a loud, "Love you, baby," from her spot under the table where she was still hiding.

Cris threw his head back and laughed before saying, "Love you too, baby!" He continued ranting. "Look, I am sure the proper authorities will sort this out, and they will see we had no choice but to do what needed to be done." Cris gestured the ax towards the now dead Mark, Holly, and Dustin, who were, more or less, stacked on top of each other. At that moment, Mikey decided to speak up.

"What do you mean WE?!" Mikey admonished. "We did not kill those people. You did; you fucking murdered them along with Deanne."

Cris shrugged, smirked, and defended himself by saying, "Hey, I didn't kill Dustin."

"No shit," Mikey snarked back, nearly shouting. "Holly murdered Dustin, we know that, but you murdered three people." She then immediately looked over at Jeremy, lecturing, "And how can you even think about siding with this asshole, Jeremy? You are supposed to be friends with April. Close friends even, you are her fucking dart partner." Mikey shook her head, rolling her eyes as she also shook her pointer finger at him. "Those three people are on your head too."

Before Jeremy could answer, Cris spoke up for him, "Wanna make it four bitch? Keep running your mouth."

Mikey winced as if she had been slapped. Before she could respond, Drew held up his hands in an attempt to diffuse the situation. "Alright, alright," he stated in a soothing fatherly tone. "Let's calm down; let's find a way out of here. And like Cris said, the authorities, or whoever can sort this out."

"Spoken like a fucking genius," Cris responded, almost cheering as he raised his fist in the air. Drew returned the fist raised with a hint of sarcasm and a sideways glance, "Alright, let's get out of here." Cris turned to check on the progress of the six men clearing the debris behind him, only to turn into a stiff right-hand punch that Kory threw.

Kory had listened to Cris's speech, and like everyone else not on Cris's side, he found it disgusting. The others might be intimidated by him, but Kory was not. Kory stopped digging and waited for Cris to turn around. When he did, Kory threw the most brutal punch he had ever thrown in his life. The hook connected solidly with Cris's jaw, causing the man to slightly stumble. Instead of following his blow with another one, Kory pointed his middle finger at Cris, "Fuck you, asshole."

Cris recovered rather quickly; it wasn't the first time he had been punched in the face. Cris, without saying a word, turned around, promptly gripped the ax with both hands, and, using the momentum from his complete turn, raised the ax driving the blade directly into the center of Kory's face. There was a loud wet thud as the edge pushed deeper into Kory's face. Blood shot out of the gaping wound as Cris pulled the ax free. Now with a four-inch gap in his face, Kory stared blankly ahead. Blood poured from the ax wound. Kory blinked once before Cris grabbed him by the front of his shirt and pulled him beyond where Cris was standing. Kory stumbled forward, crashing onto the pool table. He slid off and crumpled to the floor. Kory made a slight wheezing, gurgling noise before he died.

"Anyone ELSE have any bright ideas?" Cris announced loudly so all could hear. Just as he did, Jeremy started to scream.

Becka did not hear a single thing Cris had said. She was focused on the llama she happened to see standing by the arcade golf machine. Of course, she didn't understand why no one else saw the precious creature (but no one noticed that caterpillar Mikey vomited up, either). Becka gently held out her hand, surprised when the llama gently nuzzled her palm. "Oh my, aren't you adorable?" she cooed with the biggest smile.

"So are you," the llama answered.

Becka gasped. A talking llama! Well, that was indeed strange, she thought. She couldn't shake the feeling that something was not right, but that did not stop her from wanting to know what was going on. "Llamas can't talk," Becka said rather matter of factly.

"And that asshole should not be in charge," the llama said.

Becka turned her head slightly and saw that Cris was talking. She turned back to the llama, "Yeah, but he has the ax and the gun; he can pretend to be in charge until it's time to go. I'm okay with that."

"Go?" the llama inquired. "Where do you plan on going?"

"Why, out of here silly." Becka giggled.

"Well, the only way to get out of here is to get rid of him." The llama continued, "And if you want to catch him off guard, you need to take out his biggest fighter."

Becka turned her head and stared at Jeremy. The feeling of disgust began to swirl in her belly. That man sided with Cris and not his good friend and teammate April. She shook her head, scrunched her face, and balled up her fist. Becka looked back over at the llama and asked, "Are you sure?" The llama lifted its head, smiled at Becka, and began to fade from existence. Just before it vanished, she heard the llama say one last thing, "Take the big guy out, and you will be in charge!"

It was at that moment that Kory punched Cris. Everyone was so focused on the mini melee that no one noticed Becka walk over to the pool cues. She picked a relatively short one and clutched it in her hands. Becka was barely aware of what had happened to Kory; she was focused on waiting for the opportunity to strike Jeremy. As luck would have it, Jeremy passed right by her and the pool cue stand. Walking over towards him without even thinking about what she was doing, Becka lowered the pool cue tip to the ground. With her right foot, she stomped on it, breaking the tip clean off, giving her a rather menacing jagged spear-like point. She quickened her step and drove the pool cue into the right side of Jeremy's neck.

Jeremy was a reasonably tall man. He towered over everyone, but that was to his disadvantage this time because Becka's aim was true and on point. The new jagged tip she had made on the pool cue sunk effortlessly into Jeremy's neck, ripping open his jugular vein. Becka pulled it free, causing a small fountain of blood to erupt from the wound the pool cue left behind. Jeremy screamed out loud, prompting everyone to focus on him. Cris turned and watched as his most powerful supporter fell to his knees.

Still not knowing what had come over her, Becka took the blood-soaked pool cue and swung it as hard as she could at the back of Jeremy's head. The smack was loud, echoing through the bar. Jeremey fell forward onto his face, where he bled to death. In a victorious celebration, Becka raised the pool cue, "Boom motherfucker!"

Danny was still fuming over what Cris had just done to one of his best friends, but he knew directly attacking the man while he held onto the ax yielded unsavory results, but what Becka just did literally put the entire bar in a state of shock.

Cris raised his ax, "You fucking bitch, you just killed Jeremy." The shock and disbelief in his voice were puzzling. It seemed very hypocritical to everyone besides Billy, who was on Cris's side, something that Mikey called him out on earlier.

"Seriously, asshole?" Mikey called out. "You just killed like four people."

"Hey fuck you!" Cris shouted. "I am in control, and Jeremy was helping us get out of here."

Becka looked at Cris and just batted her eyelashes. This infuriated Cris and caused him to raise his ax and charge Becka.

Barb was now well past drunk when she looked over at Sherri, "You know what? Fuck this. We can take 'em."

Sherri looked a bit confused over at Barb, "Are you sure?"

Without answering her, Barb stood up, holding the empty vodka bottle in her hand like it was a club.

Drew watched as Cris charged Becka. Drew had had enough. He was not about to let this man hurt the woman he loved. He stepped up and picked up the seven-ball that was still on the pool table. With remarkable aim, he threw it at Cris. It struck Cris on the right side of his head, immediately bringing the man to a skidding stop. Drew picked up two more billiard balls, the nine and the four, and slowly made his way around the table towards Becka and Cris.

Danny watched as Cris stumbled. He decided that his time to act was right then. Without a word, he jumped up from his spot by the main entrance where he was digging and crossed the room over to Cris. Danny swiftly put his hands around Cris's waist. Cris stopped moving towards Becka and began to struggle against the man who had just grabbed his waist.

Billy fired the gun.

Gunshots in the bar were both loud and deafening. It caused everyone to jump each time. When the gun was fired, everyone stopped what they were doing, trying to figure out what had just happened. No one knew what or who had been shot until everyone noticed a large amount of blood spreading across the front of Drew's shirt.

Drew looked down. At first, he felt no pain. When he saw the bloodstain on his shirt grow in size, Drew dropped both billiard balls, turned, and reached out for Becka. Becka dropped her broken pool cue and caught him. Together they went to the ground.

Becka cradled Drew's head in her arms and began to cry, "No, no, no!"

Drew looked up at Becka and, with a weak smile, said, "I love you, babe." He began to cough violently, blood bubbling past his lips. As Becka held him, he died.

Barb was temporarily frozen when Billy fired the gun. When Drew fell to the ground, she raised the empty vodka bottle high above her head and hurled it towards Billy. The bottle struck Billy in his side, causing him to stumble slightly. He looked over and saw Barb standing behind the bar. She raised her middle finger and shouted, "Fuck you, asshole!" Billy didn't say a word; instead, he pointed the gun in her direction and pulled the trigger. The bullet ripped through Barb's left eye, killing the woman instantly. Her body collapsed on top of Sherri, sending the woman into a fit of terrified screaming.

Cris meanwhile, had taken advantage of Danny's beguilement and pushed him to the ground. Danny landed hard on his backside. As he hurried to get back on his feet, Cris made his way over to Danny's side. Cris raised the axe high above his head. He felt the rage bubbling over inside of him as he brought the blade down onto the back of Danny's neck. Danny's body once more collapsed to the floor. While Cris was aware that he had landed a fatal blow, he wanted to make a statement. Cris raised the axe again and again, each time plunging further and further through Danny's neck. Danny's head had now been completely severed from his body. It rolled a couple of feet away, leaving an intense river of blood in its wake. Cris carefully walked over to Danny's head, plucked it from the ground, and raised it high into the air.

"Okay!" He screamed, "Everybody, just chill the fuck out!"

Laura's voice came from her spot under the table. "Baby, what's going on?"

"These fucker's tried to be little insurrectionists," he shouted back, laughing. "But I think I got their fucking attention, now."

"Okay, babe," Laura responded a bit too gleefully. "We need to hurry, though; I am not feeling so good."

Cris turned and looked over his shoulder at the men still by the front door and shouted, "You heard my wife, hurry the fuck up."

Cris scanned over everyone still alive in the bar area. "You fucking idiots," he rebuked while shaking his head. He tossed Danny's head over the bar where it landed just a few feet from Sherri, sending the woman into another screaming fit.

Cris looked over at Becka, who had just stood up, staring daggers at him. Cris lowered his head and walked past her, never taking his eyes off of her as he did so. He approached Billy and held out his hand. "Gimme the gun, Billy," he ordered. Billy gave up the gun willingly. Cris turned and pointed the weapon at Becka. "Everyone pay attention!" He yelled and pulled the trigger.

Becka, not knowing quite how she did it, ducked just in time. The bullet sailed harmlessly over her head.

Stacie had watched the melee that had just occurred rather indifferent. She watched as, in a matter of minutes, four people had just died. She was still worried about Ernie, who, she thought, was trapped outside. She didn't care; she just wanted to keep to herself and get to Ernie. Stacie watched as Cris grabbed the gun and pointed it at Becka. Again, feeling numb to what was happening, she did not listen to what Cris said, nor did she hear the gunshot.

However, when Becka ducked the bullet, it passed over her harmlessly, but it struck Stacie in the throat. The pain Stacie felt as the bullet ripped through her throat was instant. Stacie reached up with her right hand and pressed up against the wound. She felt the warmth and stickiness of her blood as it flowed from the injury. As if he was an angel, she heard Ernie's voice call out above her. Stacie turned and smiled when she saw Ernie's face in the hole in the roof above where most of the debris lay in front of the main entrance. She took a couple of steps forward, all the while looking up at the man she loved. Stacie removed her hand from the wound, and blood began to flow freely down her front. She then collapsed to the ground.

Cris's eyes went wide as he realized what he had done. He handed the gun back to Billy and watched Stacie turn and walk towards the front door. Becka had stood up, and her heart sank. They watched as Stacie collapsed to the floor. Suddenly Ernie's voice rang through the bar. There were a few loud kicks, and suddenly they heard the unmistakable sound of wood starting to splinter. Becka looked up at the hole in the roof and realized that Ernie had somehow made his way upstairs.

Zach, George, Paul, and Kyle stood up once they heard Ernie kick the floorboards above them. They ran to the other side. They made it away safely just mere moments before Ernie, and a small amount of debris came crashing down into the bar.

Chapter 16: 1992-2000 - A Young Man's Malice

Zeus's entire demeanor changed after realizing he was in control and had a literal army at his command. Most of it could be attributed to his teenage angst and his rise in uncontrollable hormones. The other was that people, in general, were just horrible. Also, he was overcome with fear of the outside world. All these factors combined made for a very troubling few years.

From time to time, Zeus would still send his spores and mold tentacles down to explore and just cause mild general havoc on the bar patrons below. On his seventeenth birthday, Zeus was given a gift that made him forget about everything for a while. Zayan had hired some strange men to string wires and other things across the entirety of Zeus's home and the bar below. Zeus was commanded to stay out of sight. The men were instructed to not enter his room. In a few hours, the men were gone, and Zeus was allowed to see what had been done.

Patricia beamed at Zeus when he exited his room. He saw a new desk with a rather boxing-looking television on it. "What's that?" Zeus inquired.

"That son," Patricia answered, "is a computer."

Zeus had read about computers in his books and during his studies, but seeing one up close was a bit breathtaking. "Who gets to use it?" he asked.

Patricia smiled, looking at the petite, disfigured teen. "You do."

For the first time in a long time, Zeus felt happy. That night he played several of the preinstalled video games on the computer. Later on, he was introduced to the worldwide web. The initial dial-up sound of loud rings and pings was annoying, but he was lost in his own little world once he was online. He always managed to find time for his friends. They kept their shenanigans simple. Occasionally they would cause mild hallucinations, freaking out a bar patron or two. Sometimes they would mess with Tony by making him see a snake. Nothing ever as wrong leading to any significant level of violence. Zeus was content with his mild pranks and his presence online.

Like most teenagers, Zeus discovered pornography. While he knew he would never have the chance to properly pleasure a woman, he knew that self-pleasure was something he could indulge himself in. Zeus was always careful and never did it where Patricia would discover him. He soon found that the release was somehow keeping his angst at bay. It still did nothing to quell his feeling of superiority. So, he kept up his pranks at the bar below. This increased his sense of control, and he just felt his actions' power.

Zeus was always curious why he could do what he could do. This inspired him to research online topics such as telekinesis and psychic abilities. That was when he discovered that there were others like him. He did not come across any stories of people who communicated and controlled mold and fungal spores; he did find stories of people communicating with plants, animals, and even bacteria. Others, he found, could bend metal with their minds or even control fire. It was a world of knowledge he was excited to learn about. There was a downside, however. Every story about an individual who had a psychic gift would often end with these people being abducted by the government, labeled a freak, or murdered by an unruly mob. This did nothing for his fear of the outside world, and honestly, it just made it worse. It also angered him. Like himself, these gifts of humanity had to hide from the world, and it was wrong. Yes, he was quite the angry young man.

This anger led to him taking his first life two days after his nineteenth birthday.

Zeus himself did not physically kill his first victim, but he was directly responsible. He was sitting up in his room, overcome with a sudden manic sense of anger. With no way to truly direct it or adequately express how he felt, he did what he always did. Zeus turned to his friends. Sending some spores and a tendril of mold, he just watched the bar. Usually, many people showed up in pairs: friends, sometimes the occasional lover. One time he was even able to watch a couple have sex in one of the bar's bathrooms. Zeus was not in the mood for a prank today; he wanted to do something sinister, something horrific. He was so afraid of ordinary people, although stupid considering the amount of power he possessed had. Tonight he channeled that fear into anger and just looked for a victim.

A young man about the age of twenty-five sat at the very end of the bar. Everyone called him Steven. Steven had shown up numerous times with a cute chubby redhead on his arm, but tonight he was alone. Zeus, who had learned how to judge human emotion, could tell that Steven was depressed. Adding the tidbits of the conversation he had picked up on led Zeus to discover that the redhead, named Angela, had left him.

Steven was seated by himself at the end of the bar. He was nursing his third beer while fighting off the urge to just burst into tears when he heard a voice speak to him. "You will never find anyone like her."

Steven raised his head and looked over at Tony, who was bartending, "What did you say?" he asked.

Tony looked over at Steven, asking, "What?" He had nothing else to add because Steven clearly could tell that Tony was confused. So he just waved Tony off, who went back to serving drinks.

"It wasn't him," came the voice once more. "You know that."

Steven's eyes went wide. He was hearing voices in his head which alarmed him. He pushed the beer away from him across the bar and got up to go to the restroom.

"You know," the chorus of voices in his head continued, "she would regret leaving you if you were dead."

Steven stopped in his tracks. Sure, suicide had crossed his mind, but it was nothing more but a moment of weakness. He was confident that he did not want to die. Steven crossed the bar in seconds and was in the bathroom. He turned on the faucet and immediately splashed water onto his face. He looked into the mirror with both hands gripping either side of the sink when he heard the voices once more. "You should just go outside and just walk in front of a train. It would be painless, and it would show her."

The train tracks behind the bar had started to see a lot of traffic lately, so a train would be passing sooner than later. The voices were right. Maybe Angela would be taught a lesson. Steven looked in the mirror one last time, "Fuck it," he said aloud. Steven exited the bathroom and walked out of the bar. He traveled down the sidewalk, turned the corner, and immediately heard the train's whistle blow out its warning at a crossroad probably about four miles from the bar. "Do it," came the voices.

Steven shook his head, shrugging, "Why not?" and walked towards the train tracks.

Zeus could not believe what he was doing was actually working. He wished his windows were not covered so he could watch what was going on for himself, but instead, he sent a thin tendril of mold out of the building. From its vantage point, it was almost like having a front-row seat.

Steven sat down on the train tracks and lowered his head. He was nervous. He was afraid, but he was honestly done living. Angela was his entire reason for living, and he was fine dying this way. The train grew closer, and Steven felt the rails rumble underneath him. He heard the blare of the horn as the conductor spotted him. Steven looked over at the train and stood up. He took a deep breath, closed his eyes, and waited for the train to hit him.

Zeus watched courtesy from the tendril of mold. Steven's body was pummeled by the train. The man's body was no match for the steel behemoth as the conductor could not slow down. Steven's body practically exploded upon the impact. Arms, legs, and other parts of the viscera flew in several directions. The bits left of Steven were ground up and pulled under the train. After the train had passed, all that was left of Steven was a bloody wet spot.

Zeus was absolutely ecstatic. Zeus played the image of Steven's exploding body repeatedly in his mind. He was not surprised that this experience excited him so much that it gave him an erection. He knew he would have to kill again.

The following morning word of Steven's suicide traveled everywhere. People came and placed flowers near where he died. Zeus wore a smile through the remainder of the day. Patricia, though, watched the boy with a frown. The bar decided to close its doors out of respect for the night.

Patricia knew Zeus was becoming a man. She had told Zayan the week prior that Zeus needed to be told the truth. She realized that Zeus being cooped up in this apartment his entire life would adversely affect his mental health. At some point, Zeus would have to leave the apartment and learn the ways of the world. Patricia was aware that some would judge him, and there would be hardships. Zayan was adamant; Zeus was never allowed to leave that apartment or know the truth.

Zeus's nineteenth year came and went. He now had a high school education and learned more from the internet than the books ever taught him. He had convinced a depressed woman at the bar to take her life during that year, only she did not do so by train. Instead, she went home and overdosed on a large assortment of pills and alcohol. Zeus was disappointed that she did not respond to the mental image of the spores pushing into her mind about the train. He still felt rather pleased when he heard that she had taken her own life. Dead after all was dead. Besides those grisly deaths, he was content in causing his typical pranks. One such joke caused the old man Tony to finally quit.

Zeus was saddened when Tony left; he was one of his favorite people to watch, especially since he was so easily scared.

Three months before his twenty-first birthday, Zeus tried again to convince someone to take their own life. An older man who was just starting to become a regular at the bar everyone called Rudy. Rudy had lost nearly all his family in a house fire. He struggled to deal with the loss and chose booze and a dark bar corner as an escape. Rudy took the suggestion for suicide relatively quickly. He was also willing to step in front of a train. A passing motorist, however, saved the man. Zeus was angry but figured there would always be more potential victims. On his twenty-first birthday, Zeus took his third life.

Patricia had grown to love Zeus like a son. While her arrangement with Zayan had been very beneficial for her, she could not keep up the charade much longer. Patricia had had enough. Zayan could fire her and throw her out if he wanted, but she assumed he would not. She knew the secret Zayan wished to be kept. Zeus needed to understand the truth.

Zeus woke up and grumbled out loud. Another birthday. No doubt Patricia would make him something delicious. There would be gifts that were dropped off by Zayan. He had even heard rumors that a DVD player with a nice stack of DVD movies would be dropped off. Zayan had researched what a DVD was. While the idea of new media and movies was appealing, he was hoping he could find another victim in the bar for him to convince to kill themselves tonight. Zeus got up, quickly dressed, and walked into the front room. It was early in the morning. Before Patricia woke up and made breakfast, he hoped to surf the internet some. He was shocked to see Patricia sitting on the couch waiting for him.

Patricia stood up, "Good morning, Zeus." She motioned him to take a seat on the couch. "Sit down, dear. We need to talk."

Puzzled, Zeus walked over and sat on the couch. "What's up, Mom?"

Patricia sat down, took a deep breath, hesitated, and then blurted out, "I'm not your mother." Patricia looked over at Zeus. She wasn't sure why she was so nervous and why she just blurted out that statement. But when she saw the sly smile on Zeus's lips, she relaxed.

"I know, Mom," Zeus chuckled. "You're white as snow. I am a little on the dark side." He giggled. "But, you have always treated me like a son, so I don't mind calling you Mom." Zeus furrowed his brow and asked, "Why are we talking about this?"

"I think it is time you learn about your parents," Patricia answered. "Well, your father at least. I never met your mother."

Zeus could feel his heartbeat quicken in his chest. He always wanted to know about his father, which Patricia would avoid with a treat or a new gift. It got so bad that Zeus never brought it up again. "Ok," was all he could mutter.

Patricia smiled and looked over at him. "You have met your father," she started. "You see him every week."

Zeus's eyes went wide. He was a brilliant man. He knew precisely who she was talking about. He took his eyes off of her, glared at the floor, and asked, "Zayan?"

Zeus stood up; he did not know why he was suddenly overcome with rage. He was, and he demanded answers. "Why didn't you tell me sooner?" he asked.

Patricia stood up and walked over to him. She knew he was a man now, but his short stature made her long for the child she raised. "Because he told me not to," she answered as she hung her head down.

Suddenly long black tentacles of what appeared as filth began to emerge from under the furniture and other dark corners of the room. Patricia did not notice them until one had coiled itself around her left foot. Patricia looked down and what she saw caused her to scream. Soon her right leg was entrapped, and then both her arms were encircled at the wrists. Before she could finish her scream, Patricia was lifted in the air by her arms. The four tentacles pulled taught, suspending her in the air with her arms and legs spread outwards. "What the fuck!" she exclaimed.

Zeus turned to her, and she saw the anger in his eyes. Before she could respond, he began to yell at her. "How dare you keep that from me! My whole life trapped here from the world... treated like an animal.... like a fucking monster. Sure, you did as you were told, but you could have let me know. You both could have."

Patricia was still confused about why or how she was suspended in the air. She hardly registered a word Zeus had said. Instead, she asked, "Zeus, what is going on? What is this?"

Her questioning him made Zeus even angrier. "Did you even hear me?" he shouted. "I was locked away, lied to, because of what? Why? Was this just a job?" He shook his head and waved his hand profusely at her. "You know what..... fuck it! I was locked away like a monster. But the truth is, you and all those fucks outside, you guys are the monsters." Zeus shook his head as he turned away, holding back tears of hurt and anger.

Patricia wanted to plead with him, but she was overcome with fear. Whatever was holding her was unlike anything she had ever seen. Patricia could only utter the word "please" in a weak, fearful-sounding voice and could not fully speak a cohesive sentence, so she began to cry. Zeus had his back to her, talking to something she could not hear. "Oh my hell, guys. How strong are you?"

"Very," the chorus of voices chimed. "We never showed you because you never wanted us to."

Zeus asked menacingly, "What should I do with her?"

"Your choice," replied the voices.

Zeus turned around swiftly. What Patricia saw, or rather DIDN'T see in his eyes, truly frightened her. They were hollow and empty. In an instant the tentacles holding her tightened their grip.

Patricia tried to pull back, but whatever had a grip on her was way too strong. She felt something tear into her shoulders and knees.

Patricia began to panic as searing pain shot through her body. A loud, vile ripping sound accompanied the pain. The tentacles suddenly pulled themselves away, and Patricia fell to the ground. She landed on the carpeted floor with a muted thud.

She tried to roll herself over. When she could not, Patricia attempted to raise her arms and saw that they had been torn off at the shoulders. Patricia tried to move her legs only to discover that her legs had been amputated at the knees. She tried to scream, but could only produce a hoarse-sounding cough. Patricia looked up at Zeus as he walked over to her.

Zeus hovered over Patricia for a moment before hissing at her, "You did this!" That was the last thing Patricia heard before she took her final breath.

He could only watch with amazement when his tentacles of mold ripped Patricia apart. If Zeus had known their true power, maybe he would have done this years ago. He could have very well wound up in jail or worse. After watching the life vanish from Patricia's eyes, Zeus sat on the couch and began to think.

'What am I going to do?' He thought to himself. Zeus stared at Patricia's corpse while blood continued to spurt out of the four rough and uneven amputations when he got an idea. But first, he would have to wait for Zayan.

Zeus got off the couch, casually stepped over Patricia's corpse, and went into the kitchen to fix himself a bowl of cereal. By the time Zayan had arrived, Zeus's plan was already in the works.

Zayan let himself in. He had two bags of food and still needed to bring inside the DVD player and the box of DVDs. As he walked up the stairs, he called out for Patricia. When Patricia didn't answer, he made his way towards the kitchen. That was when he saw Zeus sitting on the couch next to Patricia's mutilated body.

"Hello, father," Zeus greeted him with disgust in his voice. "We need to talk."

Without a word, Zayan dropped the bags he was holding. He turned to run only to feel something coil around his feet, tripping him. Zayan's chin connected with the hard floor, dazing him for a moment. He was conscious enough to be aware that he was being dragged by whatever had him by the ankles. Abruptly, Zayan was yanked into the front room and pulled high into the air, hanging upside down. As soon as his vision had cleared, he found himself staring into the disfigured face of his son.

"S-o-o-o-n-n-n," Zayan stammered with a tremble in his voice. "I ...c..a...n .... ex..pl...ain."

"SAVE IT!" Zeus retorted. "And quit acting like a bitch. I'm not gonna kill you. I need you. See, I get why you locked me away. I do. People are just so horrible. I know that you would have been an outcast; I would have probably been bullied to death. I look like a monster, but they are monsters. So here's the deal, dad. You keep paying the bills. You keep dropping off food. You keep bringing me what I need, and I will stay here."

Zayan, who was trembling uncontrollably, glanced over at Patricia's corpse. Zeus noticed the fear in his father's eyes and smiled. "She will stay with me. I need her.... for my friends."

Zayan looked back over at Zeus and could not believe what he saw. Tentacles of what appeared to be black filth looked to be growing from his back. Not wanting to be in the apartments any longer, Zayan agreed, "Ok, Ok, let me go."

Zeus smiled, "No, no, you need to listen. You will drop things off for me at the landing every week. In return, I will leave a new list. You will retrieve the list, then you leave. You better get whatever is on that list, or well, I will venture out of this place. And I don't think you want people to know about your monster in the apartments." Zeus tilted his head back and laughed a sinister laugh.

Zayan closed his eyes and found himself crashing to the floor. He was on his feet in a flash, running towards the door. Zayan was in the stairwell rushing downstairs when he heard Zeus call after him. "Don't forget the DVD player and movies."

Zayan ran out the door and into the street. He bolted to his car and jumped in behind the wheel. He was about to start the engine when he realized what had just happened. If he left now, what would stop his son from leaving the apartments and massacring a group of people like he did Patricia. Worse yet, what if his son was caught? He would be exposed for what he had done. After a few deep breaths, Zayan exited his car, went to his trunk, and got the DVD player along with the box of assorted DVDs. He walked back to the apartment door and let himself in. Zayan placed the boxes on the landing of the stairs, where he found there was already a list waiting for him. After a quick peruse, he realized he could easily manage this request. He folded the list and placed it into his pocket. He thought to himself all he had to do was keep doing what he had been doing for the past twenty-one years.

The next three years went by at an average pace. Zeus's lists would become elaborate, with more mature tastes. Zayan kept finding ways to meet them. A couple of unexplained deaths appeared to be accidental that occurred near the bar. Zayan knew what had really happened, but he did not care. It was either this or be exposed for the crimes he had committed. He felt guilt from those, but now, he was also guilty of taking care of a literal monster in his apartment.

Zeus loved his new arrangement. He stopped cleaning, and for a good reason. Before he knew it, he was entirely surrounded by friends. Unfortunately, he was growing bored. Weeks before his twenty-fifth birthday, he made a very sinister request from Zayan. That is when everything changed.

Chapter 17: 2022 - Fighting Back Up

As April started walking towards the stairs, both Jennifer and Nikole stayed where they were for the moment. They were honestly too scared to move. In just a little over an hour, darkness engulfed them, and three of their friends were brutally murdered by what seemed to belong to black tendrils of filth. And to make matters worse, April's entire demeanor had changed. Gone was the empathetic woman who would give you the shirt off of her back. Instead, a hardened-hearted individual replaced her.

Nikole reached up to the cheek her mother had just slapped and rubbed it slightly. "Have you ever seen my mother like this?"

Jennifer shook her head slowly before answering, "No, never; whatever happened upstairs has her pissed off."

April, who was not entirely out of earshot, heard bits and pieces of what her daughter said. The truth was that April was acting a bit different and did not feel like her usual self. She knew it, but she had just witnessed several people she cared about die, not to mention both of her children were in harm's way. She had every right to feel unlike herself. Instead of admonishing her daughter, April turned around and raised her voice slightly. "Will you two hurry up?" she called over to them. At that moment, two gunshots rang out, followed by a third, directly overhead, assuming in the bar upstairs. "We have to get up there now!" she intensely screamed.

Nikole and Jennifer quit their discussion and began to walk over towards April. Just then, Nikole watched as another black tentacle surged through to where her mom was standing. "Mom!" Nikole shrieked as she pointed in the direction of the tentacle.

April turned, seeing the snakelike mass of filth as it rushed towards her. She had no idea what the stuff was, but she had a hunch that it would not appreciate her homemade torch. April gripped the flaming table leg tightly, deciding now was the time to go on the offensive. Without warning, she charged the tentacle. Nikole was shocked to see her mom rush towards their adversary with such reckless abandon. When April swung her torch in the direction of the tentacle, it immediately caught fire.

"Holy Shit!" Jennifer exclaimed. "Did you see how easy that shit caught on fire?" She began to say something else, but instead of being able to get out a cohesive word, all she could blurt out was a wet-sounding "Urk."

Nikole quickly spun around. She saw that another tentacle had emerged from behind them. It had wrapped itself around Jennifer's neck and the lower half of her face, ultimately preventing her from breathing. Nikole raised her torch, ready to strike, but before she could, Jennifer had hit the tip of the tentacle with her own torch. Instantly the alien's appendage caught fire. Flames ran up the length of the tentacle and both women assumed that the creature would relinquish its hold on Jennifer. Instead, the tentacle held fast to Jennifer's neck and face. Jennifer's eyes widened and she attempted to scream as she felt the heat from the spreading flame on her cheeks. Nikole watched in horror as Jennifer's hair caught fire.

The pain of the flames was intense. Jennifer dropped her torch and began to slap at the flaming tentacle with her bare hands. Her strikes were weak, and the tentacle only squeezed tighter rather than let go. The pain of the spreading fire began to drift away as the lack of oxygen from the tentacle's grip caused Jennifer to pass out.

April struck the approaching tentacle once more. With that blow, the tentacle, now with a flaming tip, retreated further into the basement. It slammed itself onto the ground in an effort to put out the fire that covered it. Even though it was dark, April could still see where it had gone because the tip had a faint red glow from where she had burned it. Nikole suddenly produced a guttural scream, diverting April's attention away from the fleeing tentacle.

When April looked over, she saw Jennifer's head completely engulfed in flames while Nikole was beating at a tentacle that looked like it was growing out of the back of Jennifer's head. Jennifer's torch had fallen to the ground. Flames were starting to spread across the dance floor. April ran over to try and help Nikole free Jennifer when the tip of the tentacle separated from the rest. The tentacle, minus its tip, fled to the back of the basement.

Jennifer, whose head was still burning, collapsed face first to the floor. April dropped her torch and tried to catch Jennifer, but all she managed to do was soften the blow as both women landed on the floor together. Thinking quickly, April pulled Jennifer's shirt up off of her back and over her head in an attempt to smother the flames. Once April put the flames out, she peeled back the shirt with trembling, burnt hands. There was a sickening tearing sound as most of Jennifer's scorched scalp started peeling away from her skull with the shirt. Red and black blistering skin with patches of white skull underneath glared up at April. Upon seeing the remainder of Jennifer's skull, April turned her head and gagged. Holding her breath and squinting down at Jennifer's now motionless body, April pulled the shirt back up over Jennifer's head.

"Is she?" Nikole started to ask.

Shaking with anger, April stood up but not before gathering her and Jennifer's torches. April squinted her eyes and scanned the dark recesses in the bar basement that the glows of their torches did not quite reach. She let out a scream and heaved into the back of the basement the torch that was initially hers. Both women watched the torch sail through the air. When it hit the ground, chasing away the shadows, there were no black tentacles around. The wall next to the torch started to catch fire, but at this point, April didn't care. She just wanted out of this basement. April also knew there were two suitably-sized fire extinguishers upstairs. The torch indeed would not cause that much damage in the short time she believed it would take her to subdue Cris. "Run for the stairs," April commanded. She turned and ran for the stairwell with Nikole following close behind.

As April started to climb the stairs, another gunshot rang out above them. Not too long after, another gunshot rang out. "Move your ass, Nikole," April ordered as they climbed the stairs, still holding their torches. Nikole was keeping pace with her mother when all of a sudden, one of the tentacles popped out between one of the stairs' open slats and wrapped itself around Nikole's ankle. Nikole screamed and began to strike the tentacle with her torch. Flames quickly spread as April awkwardly stumbled down the stairs to help her daughter. April began to beat at the tentacle wrapped around Nikole's ankle without hesitation. "Let go of my fucking daughter!" April screamed.

Nikole had tears of anger, fear, and pain flooding down her cheeks. She was not about to let what had killed her friends kill her. Without notice, she felt the thing around her leg start to loosen as the flames began to spread downwards on the tentacle. "Mom, it's letting go!" Nikole screamed excitedly. April thrust her torch down and felt the tentacle slide away as it let go of Nikole's legs. It retreated underneath the stairwell. April lost her grip on her torch and watched it fall after the tentacle. She grabbed her daughter, "You ok, baby?"

"It burns, but I'll live," Nikole sobbed with relief.

"Ok, let's go!" April sighed and turned towards the door at the top of the stairs.

Just as she did, there was the sound of something sliding in the front of the door. Unexpectedly the door was flung open. Standing in the doorway was her son Christian. He looked down at his mom. April could see that he had blood splatter on his face and was breathing heavily. "Mom, get up here now!" he shouted at her. "All hell has broken loose."

April did not say a word; instead, she grabbed her daughter by the hand that was not holding the torch and pulled her forwards. Just before the women made it to the top of the stairs, Cris appeared from out of nowhere behind Christian.

Cris was raising the ax above his head.

Chapter 18: 2022 - Straight In and Straight Out

As Ernie crashed through the floor, everyone all at once turned in his direction. Cris winced when he heard Ernie's anguished screams as he crawled over towards Stacie's body.

"No, no, no," Ernie sobbed, rolled onto his butt, and scooped Stacie's bloody corpse up into his arms. He cradled her head against his chest and brushed her hair out of her face. "Wake up, baby, wake up," he pleaded.

Cris's heart hurt for Ernie. The bullet was meant for Becka. He liked Ernie, and Stacie was being so compliant. She was staying out of the way, not causing any problems. She was indeed an innocent bystander.

"Goddamnit, Becka!" Cris yelled. "You couldn't just stand still and let me shoot you. Stacie's blood is on your hands." He got a tight grip on his ax and walked over to Becka. "Well, looks like it's the old-fashioned way for you."

Becka was lost in thought, not looking in Cris's direction. Instead, she was staring down at Drew. As Cris started to walk towards her, Becka knelt down and rested her head on Drew's chest as fresh tears streamed down her face. Mikey watched as Cris stalked his way over to Becka. It was at that moment she had had enough. Mikey quickly made her way around the pool table, finding her way between Cris and Becka. She stood her ground with her arms outstretched, shielding Becka from him.

"Move, Mikey!" Cris demanded.

"Fuck you," Mikey said defiantly.

Brett and A.J. had stopped digging and were now watching the commotion. Brett slowly reached into the top pocket of his cargo pants. He carefully removed the flip-open pocket knife he always carried there. Brett had a feeling that he was going to have to fight A.J., or that's what the voices he had been hearing were telling him. Brett hadn't heard the voice until after Becka killed Jeremy, but the voices were enough to keep him on his toes. Also, as he looked at A.J., he had noticed that A.J.'s face had begun to change into something demonic.

A.J. had picked up a two by four with a jagged edge and was holding it in his right hand, lowered but ready to strike. He wasn't too worried about what was going on in the bar. Cris was a dear friend, and A.J. knew he would no doubt make it out safe. However, he had started to hear voices. These voices were telling him that he should kill Brett. In addition, every time he locked eyes with Brett, the man's eyes would change to black voids, and scales would flutter into existence on his skin. A.J. knew the confrontation was coming, but he wanted to see what was about to happen for now. While all eyes were on Cris, A.J. noticed that Eric had let go of Hope and was now making a move towards Billy.

Mikey's direct defiant act in the face of Cris was precisely the distraction Eric needed. If Mikey had the confidence to do what she was doing, then he could easily take down the little pissant he once called friend. Eric was around the other end of the pool table and closed the short distance between himself and Billy within seconds. Billy saw Eric coming and spun around quick enough to aim the gun at Eric and pull the trigger. The bullet hit Eric right between the eyes, taking the back part of his skull off. Eric's momentum drove him forward, and his body came to a skidding halt at Billy's feet.

Hope lost it. She began to scream so hysterically loud that it hurt Cris's ears. Cris stepped back and looked over at her, yelling, "Oh for fuck's sake, Hope, shut the fuck up!" But she did not; instead, she began to scream a series of nonsensical words over and over. Cris shook his head, looked over at Billy, and ordered, "Man, handle the bitch out of my misery."

Like an obedient servant, Billy raised the gun and pulled the trigger. The bullet struck Hope in the left temple and exited through her right cheek, killing her instantly. Cris turned around and faced Mikey again. "Move; I don't want to hurt you," he demanded.

"Are you fucking kidding me right now?" Mikey asked, clearly exasperated. "You've fucking slaughtered people left, right, and sideways and you don't want to hurt me?" Mikey then reached up and pinched the bridge of her nose. "You are so fucking stupid," she continued. "Look around you, dumbass. Over half of the people you called friends or played against are dead. Because of you!"

Cris began to shake his head, "Because of me?" he guffawed. "No, this is April's fault. Every bit of it. She had her moment. These deaths are on her hands. Yeah, I had to kill them, but I was defending myself."

"You pushed a woman down the stairs for saying you had a limp dick," Mikey retorted.

"My husband's dick is not limp; he is rock hard!" Laura shouted from her place under the table.

"Thanks, babe!" Cris shouted back.

Laura cheered out, "Woot woot."

"Oh my fucking God!" Mikey screamed while staring at the ceiling, "You're both fucking nuts."

Before Cris could respond to Mikey's accusation, George and Paul left Zach's side and walked over. Cris readied the ax thinking they were coming for him, but what they did next shocked everyone. Both men grabbed Mikey by her arms and jerked her towards the wall near the arcade golf machine.

"What the fuck, guys!" Zach shouted.

"He's right, man," Paul answered.

"Yeah, sorry, brother," George spoke. "I mean, April caused this. Ok, this is fucking survival."

"We have only been trapped in this bar for a couple of hours now. What the fuck do we need to survive?" Zach questioned, realizing he had just asked the question of the night. "Sure, the roof caved in. We had three accidental deaths here. But what the fuck are we fighting for?" He then gestured over to the door. "Look, that's just wood, and if that asshole," as he pointed towards Cris, "had used the ax on any of the beams and not on people, we would probably be out of here!"

"Shut the fuck up, loser," Jason shouted from behind Billy. "Jesus, look, we all want out, but that doesn't change the fact that none of us would be here if April left those doors closed. Kevin, Lori, and hell, that dumb fuck Paco would still be alive. So, hey, if bloods gotta be shed to prove a point, so be it."

"Oh my God," Zach shouted. "You're all fucking nuts."

Cris walked over towards Becka this entire time, not taking his eyes off Zach. "You sit down and shut up, or you're next." He then looked down at Becka, "Face me bitch."

Becka turned around and looked up at Cris, tears flowing down her cheeks. She looked up at Cris's face. A smile tugged on her lips. In seconds she began to laugh hysterically. Becka was still hallucinating and what she saw was not Cris, but the head of a penis stretched comically wide and drooping over slightly to one side on a rather pathetic-looking neck. "Oh my God, you ARE a dickhead," Becka snorted as she continued to laugh.

Cris's eyes went wide, and in one smooth stroke, he raised the ax then brought it down into the center of Becka's chest. Becka still continued to laugh. Cris pulled the ax free and brought it down once more on her chest. Blood bubbled from Becka's mouth as warm blood sprayed from the now gaping hole between her breasts. She felt herself choking on her as darkness started to cloud over her vision. With her last ounce of strength, Becka looked up at Cris and said, "You are a limpdick pussy boy." With her final act of defiance complete she collapsed onto Drew's body and died.

Before Cris brought the ax down a second time onto Becka, Sara made her way over to Lucy and Christian. She spun Christian around and demanded, "Why don't you give me that knife?"

Lucy stepped between them, "Bitch, what is your fucking problem? We're supposed to be friends."

Sara looked Lucy up and down, "Bitch please; I only side with winners; plus, you're just a basic hoe, so give me the fucking knife." It was at that moment Lucy snapped.

Lucy turned towards Christian and snatched the knife from his hands. In one swift motion, she turned and began to thrust the knife repeatedly into Sara's stomach. The blade protruded completely through Sara's body and out of her back twice. Right before Becka took her last breath, Lucy had driven the knife six times into Sara's thin abdomen. Lucy stepped back and watched with a sinister smile on her face as Sara frantically pressed her hands against her stomach, trying to keep her blood and intestines inside her. Slowly, Sara turned towards Jason. She took a step towards him before collapsing on the floor and died seconds later with her blood pooling from underneath her.

Christian took that moment to pounce. Jason stood directly behind Billy, almost acting like a silent sentry guardian at the basement door. When Jason watched as his girlfriend was brutally stabbed to death in front of him, his guard was completely down. Christian lowered his shoulder and charged Jason. He connected with Jason's midsection and sent the man careening into Billy, sending both men to the floor. Christian grabbed the table blocking the door with both of his hands, and slid it out of the way.

Cris, covered in Becka's blood, turned around just as Billy and Jason fell to the floor. He watched as Christian flung open the door to the basement and quickly stomped over in that direction.

Ernie stood up just as Cris made his approach towards Christian. He was seething with rage. He looked around the room. Ernie saw Kyle standing by himself near the electric slot machines. "Hey, Kyle," Ernie called out. "Help me get that cocksucker."

Kyle locked eyes with Ernie. All the anger he felt from Cris killing his friends welled up inside his mind. "Yeah, let's get that fuckboy." Both men charged towards Cris just as he raised the ax above Christian's head.

Christian was shocked to see his mother and sister near the top of the stairs. "Mom, get up here!" He shouted, "All hell has broken loose."

April looked up and was relieved to see her son, Christian, waiting at the top of the stairs. She grabbed Nikole by the hand and ran up the stairs when she saw Cris appear, seemingly from nowhere, behind Christian. Slowly Cris raised the axe, and before April had time to scream, she watched in horror as Cris brought the axe down, swiftly. There was a loud wet thumping noise as the axe was planted into the back of Christian's skull. Moments later but what felt like an eternity to April, Cris pulled the axe free. Blood started to drain from the back of Christian's head. He collapsed at Cris's feet and blood began to pool under his head. April screamed for her son as she watched his blood trickle down the stairs and let go of Nikole's hand. She was at her son's side in a flash, but by the time she got her hands on him, he was dead.

April glared up at Cris, who was now smiling. "Come on then, Bitch," he taunted before he was suddenly shoved violently to his left by both Ernie and Kyle. April stood up and ran out the door, with Nikole following close behind. As they exited the basement, what April saw was nothing less than pure pandemonium.

Chapter 19: 202 2- A Second Deadly Rumble

April did a complete circle to scan her bar. What she saw was both heartbreaking and horrific. Bodies of people she called friends before patrons were lying on the ground. She glanced to her right to see Zach walking over towards George and Paul, who appeared to be holding Mikey back against her will. April turned and observed A.J. and Brett circling each other, seemingly preparing for battle. She watched Laura crawling out from under a table. Laura was reaching out blindly towards Lucy as Lucy was on her knees crying, holding her bloody hands up to her mouth. Lucy was, no doubt, in shock after watching her boyfriend get his head split open. April noticed a butcher's knife on the ground in front of Lucy. She looked over towards the second entrance by the ruined dartboard. Both Ernie and Kyle were getting ready to fight Cris, who had the Ax raised. April realized right then who was responsible for all this. Rage and pure hatred flooded her soul. Before she knew it, April walked over, scooped the bloody butcher knife off the floor, and made her way over to help Ernie and Kyle subdue Cris.

Nikole followed her mom out of the basement. As she looked behind her, she was shocked to see how much the fire they had caused downstairs had spread. Yes, they had left torches downstairs — one at the back of the basement and the one that fell under the stairs. The wood had to be old and dry because the fire spread like wildfire as flames were devouring the bottom part of the stairs. Nikole wondered how long they had before the entire bar would be engulfed in flames. However, she did not have time to worry about it at that exact moment because Billy was on his feet. He raised the gun when he saw Nikole standing there with the torch in her hands.

As soon as April emerged from the basement, Brett flipped out the six-inch blade of his pocket knife and readied himself for an attack. A.J. heard the sound of the blade clicking open, turned, and asked, "Whatcha doin' mate?"

"You know what I'm doing," Brett answered.

A.J. snickered, "Suppose I do." He raised the jagged two by four up, "Well, let's have at it then."

The men circled each other momentarily, utterly unaware of what was happening around them. Without warning, Brett stabbed forward with his knife while A.J. stabbed downward with his jagged piece of wood. Brett kept good care of his knife; it was sharp and slid easily into A.J.'s ample belly. A.J.'s aim, though, was accurate and the jagged piece of wood he was holding sunk halfway into Brett's neck. The pain was intense, and Brett felt it in his teeth. Brett went down to one knee seething but did not let go of his knife. He grabbed his weapon with both hands and effortlessly slid it sideways, slicing A.J. open. A.J. screamed as he felt the knife cut his flesh open. In response, A.J. pushed the piece of wood deeper into Brett's neck. Brett felt his vision darken as blood flowed around the wood in his neck A.J. pulled the jagged two-by-four piece free, causing blood to erupt from Brett's ruined neck like a geyser. Knowing he was going to die, Brett made one last final push with his knife and finished slicing open A.J.'s stomach. Brett fell over and died just as A.J. tried to take a step back and examine his wound. A.J.'s intestines suddenly unraveled from the near two-foot gash on his stomach. A.J. stood wavering, watching the blood and guts spill from his body before collapsing forward on top of his internal organs.

Zach walked over to Paul and spun the man around. Without saying a word, Zach punched his friend in the face. "The fuck?" Paul asked, bewildered. Zach threw another punch before he could say another word, this time slamming his fist into Paul's nose.

Mikey took advantage of the situation and immediately formed a fist with her free left hand and punched George directly in his face. George let go of her and stumbled back. She had connected with his nose, and tears welled in his eyes. Blood trickled out of his left nostril. "Bitch," he cried. Mikey balled up her fists, held them up, and smiled. "Bring it, pussy," she teased. George let out a strange howl and ran at Mikey. Mikey tried to punch at George, but he was too fast. Before she knew what was happening, George lifted her high into the air and slammed her head first onto the arcade golf machine. There was a loud, sickening crack as the screen of the golf machine imploded. Glass shards from the screen embedded themselves in the side of Mikey's head as her skull slightly caved in. Still conscious, Mikey struggled to get back on her feet but fell to her side. She rolled over on her back and tried to gasp for air. Before she lost consciousness, she could see George standing over her as he raised his right foot.

Zach turned the moment he noticed Mikey hit the ground. "Mikey!!" he shouted. Paul took advantage of the situation and landed a perfect one-two punch to the side of Zach's face. Zach stumbled for a minute before landing on his bottom. Zach looked over towards Mikey just in time to see George raise his foot before stomping it down into the center of Mikey's face. Zach turned away and closed his eyes as he heard George stomp the ground two more times. Then, something that sounded like it was made of metal skittered over to the floor next to him.

Laura had made her way out from under the table. Although she was blind, she found Lucy with ease, thanks to the young woman's loud sobbing. With fights breaking out around them and bodies falling to the floor, no one noticed when Laura grabbed Lucy by the hair and pulled her under the table. Lucy was still sobbing when Laura positioned herself on top of Lucy. She blindly felt her hands around

Lucy's face. When she found what she was looking for, she extended her thumbs and drove them deep into Lucy's eyes. Lucy began to scream and thrash against Laura. Laura pressed harder, putting all her weight behind her thumbs. Thick blackish-red blood flowed from Lucy's destroyed eye sockets. Laura's thumbs pushed their way through Lucy's orbital muscles and into Lucy's brain, killing the young woman. Laura slowly removed her thumbs and smiled when she heard the sickening pop her thumbs made as she pulled them free.

When Nikole saw Billy raise the gun, she swung her torch at him. The blunted flaming end struck Billy square in the chest with enough force that he dropped the gun. Nikole went to raise it again, but Jason, who was finally getting off the floor from when Christian knocked him down, jumped up and caught the base of the torch with both of his hands and pushed it backward. Billy stepped forward to help Jason with Nikole, but a loud shrill, near inhuman-sounding scream, erupted behind the bar. Billy froze where he was at, which happened to be in front of the entryway to the basement where the door was still flung open and black smoke was now billowing out as flames tore their way through the basement.

Sherri was on the verge of passing out. She had stayed on the ground from behind the bar and had found another bottle of alcohol. This time it was a slim twenty-ounce bottle of cinnamon whiskey, and she was now very drunk. Sherri was oblivious to what was going on behind her. She knew it was terrible, but she did not care. She was more than ten sheets to the wind. Unexpectedly the floor underneath her started to grow warm. Sherri was unaware that a fire was now raging in the basement as it quickly burned through the old wood paneling and floors that were down there. To her, the heat was unnatural. She felt like a portal to hell was about to open up underneath her. She leaped to her feet in her drunken state and screamed like a banshee. Unaware of what she was doing, she ran around the corner of the bar and towards what she thought was an open door. She did not know it was the door to the basement or that Billy was standing there until she collided with him.

Billy's mind did not register what was happening or who was charging him until Sherri slammed into him, sending both of them tumbling backward into the flaming basement. Now weakened because of the fire, the stairs quickly collapsed as Billy and Sherri fell through them and slammed into the burning floor below. Thankfully for Sherri, the impact and the exuberant amount of alcohol she drank rendered her unconscious, meaning she did not feel pain as she burned to death. On the other hand, Billy broke both legs and felt everything as the flames began to torch his clothing first and then his flesh. He tried to scream, but the fire scorched his airway and lungs. In seconds, Billy, too, burned to death.

Jason had knocked Nikole off balance and managed to disarm her. Now holding her torch, he swung it like a bat and connected it with the side of Nikole's head. Nikole's ears started to ring, and she stumbled backward. She collided with a chair and landed on her stomach. She saw her mother was almost ready to join Ernie and Kyle as they fought Cris. Nikole opened her mouth and screamed, "Mom, help!" The very next moment, Jason raised the torched high in the air and slammed it down into the back of her head. There was a loud wet smack. April turned just in time to see Jason bring the torch down onto the back of Nikole's head once more, this time delivering a killing blow.

April completely lost her mind. In just a mere matter of minutes, she personally watched her two children get brutally murdered in nearly the same fashion. April let out a gut-wrenching scream. With the butcher knife in her hand, she ran towards Jason. Jason raised the torch, ready to strike, but April was on top of him before he could. Jason felt being slammed up against the pool table, falling backward on top of it. April brought the knife down, slamming it through Jason's cheek. She pulled the weapon free and stabbed down again. The knife went through the soft skin on the side of Jason's neck. April pulled it free just as two shots rang out in front of her. Instead of looking up, she slammed the knife down again into Jason's left eye. Jason found enough strength to push April, who was now standing to the side of the pool table, away. He rolled over and crashed to the floor at April's feet. Blood flowed from his wounds as he tried to crawl away, but April was a woman possessed. She knelt onto Jason's back and began to repeatedly stab the man in his back ten more times before she heard Zach calling out for her to stop.

April's scream caused Kyle to turn his head. That was all the distraction Cris needed. Cris swung the ax sideways with near inhuman reflexes, and the Ax's blade buried itself into Kyle's face just above his nose and under his eyes. Ernie watched as Cris pulled the ax free. Ernie wanted vengeance. He struck out a powerful right jab connecting with Cris's right cheek just as Kyle's body fell forward, blood flowing from the gash on his face.

"Put down the ax and fight me, fair motherfucker," Ernie demanded.

Cris did not respond to Ernie. Cris spun in a complete circle, starting with the force from Ernie's punch. He had the ax leveled. Cris used this speed and momentum as the ax swung freely. He slammed the ax into Ernie's rib cage. Ernie choked and wheezed as blood bubbled out of his mouth, but he showed no fear. Instead, Ernie swung out at Cris. Cris ducked the weakened blow effortlessly. Ernie crashed onto a heap of the rubble by the second entrance. "Dammit, Ernie!" Cris said. "Look. I am sorry about Stacie. Fuck man, this truly sucks." Cris then raised the ax above his head. "Go be with your woman," Cris stated as he brought the ax down into the back of Ernie's head. At that instant, two gunshots rang out from the bar area.

Cris situated himself and looked for his wife. He found her covered in blood, sitting on Lucy's body underneath one of the high tables by the dartboards. He quickly rushed over to her and helped her to her feet.

"Baby that you?" Laura asked.

"Yeah," he said. "Now, let's go over there and finish this."

Zach opened his eyes and realized that what had slid over to him was Kevin's gun. Billy must have dropped it. He looked over at it and was able to quickly wrap his hands around it. Paul had turned his back on him and was now walking over to his brother kneeling next to Mikey.

"Is she dead?" Paul asked.

"I caved her fucking head in like a watermelon," George answered gleefully, "Of course, she is fucking dead."

Zach got to his feet and looked at the chaos and carnage around him. He saw Sherri and Billy topple into the basement that was now billowing smoke at an alarming rate. He saw Jason assaulting Nikole. Zach heard April scream as she swiftly appeared out of nowhere and tackled Jason into the pool table. He looked down at the gun in his hands and realized he now had the power to truly end this. Zach was not quite sure how many bullets were left in the gun, but he had a chance to end this, and he was going to take it, but first, he had to do something. Zach took a step towards George and Paul, who were laughing over Mikey's corpse, and without saying a word, Zach raised the gun and pulled the trigger, shooting Paul in the back of the head. Paul's body fell forward, collapsing onto Mikey.

George raised his hands in defense, about to say something. Zach didn't want to hear it. He quickly and wordlessly raised the gun, shooting George in the center of his forehead. George's body had not hit the ground before Zach had turned and ran over to April, now soaked in Jason's blood as she repeatedly sunk the butcher knife she was holding into the dead man's ruined chest cavity.

"April!" Zach shouted. "April, stop. He's fucking dead."

April raised the knife, looked up at Zach, and saw that he was now in possession of Kevin's gun. Zach looked down at her, and his heart broke. She was drenched in blood. He could tell that the April he knew was not the person looking up at him. This woman was angry. Slowly, he helped her to her feet.

Cris walked into the main bar area leading his wife. Kicking the basement door closed as he went to avoid the smoke billowing out. "Billy, my man is that...." He stopped when he saw April and Zach standing by the pool table, the gun in Zach's hand. "Fuck no!" he screamed. "Fuck, no!" Cris did not like losing and what was happening right now was not good for him. "No, no, no. Me and my wife are getting out of here, bitch." He pushed Laura behind him and raised the ax. "I am still in control!" Cris finished as he walked to the other side of the pool table.

"Over my dead body," April growled. Then with no warning, she launched herself across the pool table towards Cris.

Chapter 20: 2001-2022 - Everything Under His Control

The deal between Zeus and Zayan went better than Zeus expected. Like clockwork, Zayan would drop off the provisions Zeus required in the spot Zeus had indicated every week. Just as Zeus stated, there was always a list left behind. There was always an odd item also on this list. Sometimes it was a small appliance, sometimes an electronic device, or the occasional book. It was never something Zayan could not or would not acquire until three years into their mutual agreement, nearly a month after Zeus turned twenty-eight.

Zeus was enjoying his days hidden away from the world. He was immune to the evils just outside his door. However, those underneath him were not in any way resistant to him. He was still up to his typical mischievous actions for the past three years. Zeus no longer called his antics pranks. He considered them deeds. He felt that he was simply defending himself or others for every person he convinced to kill themselves. In his mind, no one is innocent. Whatever damage he caused was justified. No one was there to tell him otherwise. But he had started to grow bored. Sure he knew he was responsible for the suicides he had caused, but the rush and thrill were no longer there. It was barely enough to quell his sociopathic and psychopathic behavior. Nothing quite matched the exhilaration he had felt when he ripped Patricia limb from limb. He did try other things to get his adrenaline up. He influenced two more men to fight, leading to a knife being pulled and one man being stabbed to death. He saw it all through the eyes of the man doing the stabbing, thanks to the ability he discovered he had while controlling his fungal spores. The scene he witnessed was all blurry, though. Even the bits he caught from the tendril of mold he had sitting outside watching didn't really do anything for him. Sure it was a bit of a rush. But he needed more. He yearned to feel the pleasure of killing someone himself. Zeus was obsessed by that rush. Shortly after he turned twenty-eight, he asked Zayan for a whore.

Zayan read the note; there were, of course, the primary food requests, a few new DVD movies, but at the very end of the list was the word whore. Zeus included a list of requirements along with the word. The whore must be female. She had to be someone no one would miss. Under no circumstances was Zayan to tell her anything about him. After reading the note, Zayan was baffled, "I don't know where to get a whore!"

Two tentacles of mold slithered down the hallway with lightning quickness. They stopped inches away from Zayan's face. He heard Zeus' voice echo through the apartment and stairwell. "You do know, and you will find me one, or else, everyone will know."

Entirely unnerved by what he was being asked to do, Zayan bolted down the stairs. Before he opened the door, Zeus' voice echoed down to him, "Remember, Dad, I own you; do what I say, and nothing will happen to you."

Zayan nervously walked to his car. The moon was high in the sky. The bar had been closed for a couple of hours now, so he was confident no one had seen him. He climbed into his car and stared forward for a few moments. He heard stories of people killing themselves on the train tracks after visiting the bar. Zayan knew that Zeus had to be somehow responsible. As long as Zayan wasn't personally involved with it, he was able to turn the other cheek. But now, Zeus wanted him to become directly involved. He was being asked to lead an innocent woman to her doom. Zayan stared out his window and up at the moon. Thinking out loud, "Well, whores aren't really innocent," he rationalized. "I mean, not the ones that are easy, or easy to find." He sat in his car for nearly thirty minutes. He finally came to the conclusion that whores weren't really people. They were just empty shells of a woman ready to die. With that justification setting his mind at ease, Zayan drove off preparing himself to fulfill Zeus' list.

That week Zayan went about his everyday tasks. He was also able to acquire everything Zeus had asked for except for the whore. He would have to find her the night of his actual delivery to Zeus. Zayan had done some research and found that a couple of places near him had a very seedy nightlife. One such place was in downtown Sandwich, Illinois. There was a grocery store that was busy during the day. At night, the alleyway behind it was populated by women of the night. It was not a place Zayan knew about personally, but people talked, and he listened. That first night was absolutely nerve-racking, but it did become a place he would often revisit over the next several years.

Zayan thought it best not to use his own personal vehicle. He did not want anyone to recognize his car if someone saw him driving behind the grocery store at night. Instead, he rented a car for the evening. Zayan figured he would have to pick wisely but only because he did not know what kind of shape Zeus was in. He had not physically seen the man in three years, so he figured the more frail-looking woman, the better. He also figured that a drug addict would not be missed and that her disappearance would go unnoticed. The whore's name was Cindy. She was what most men would call petite. Her face was shrunk in. Her looks made it obvious that she chose the prostitution lifestyle to fuel an unhealthy drug addiction. Cindy sauntered over towards Zayan. After a brief nervous exchange, she entered the car. Zayan told her he was driving her back to his apartment. This whore was quite a chatterbox. She went on and on about things Zayan did not actually hear. He was in his own head, bathed in guilt. He knew he was delivering this woman to her death. Zayan hoped that Zeus only wanted the woman for carnal pleasure. But as he recalled the state of Patricia's body and how Zeus went about in such an effort to scare him, he felt otherwise. Not to mention the rash of suicides that had taken place on the train tracks behind the bar. Zayan knew Zeus had to have had a hand in those. Most of the town figured that depressed people got more depressed while drinking and that those suicides were the rash decisions of desperate men and women. Not Zayan; he knew better.

When they arrived at the apartment, Zayan opened his car door. He started to go around to the other side and let Cindy out, but she was out before he got there. Puzzled, she looked at him and laughed, "Oh honey, you ain't got to be no gentleman to me." She smiled a crooked tooth smile at him. "As long as the money is good, Imma fuck you for however long you want."

Zayan just nodded, "Ok, right this way."

They walked to the doorway in silence that led to the apartments. Zayan kept his head down, hoping no one would see him. The stores around the bar were closed, but the bar was relatively busy. He made it to the door unnoticed and swung it open. "After you, dear," he said.

"Oh baby," Cindy laughed once more. "You ain't gotta be that humble."

Zayan smiled, "I'll tell you, why don't you go upstairs? There is beer in the fridge. I have to go get something out of my car."

Cindy smiled warmly back at him as she did not sense anything threatening. "Ok, you best hurry, though, because once I step foot in here, you're on the clock."

Zayan watched as Cindy walked up the stairs and then closed the door. Quickly he jogged over to his car and opened the trunk. He grabbed the bags of requested items from Zeus and then hurried back to the apartment door. He opened the door and was not surprised to see Cindy had vanished. Zayan walked up the stairs and placed the bags down on the landing. He looked down and saw a note. Setting the bag down, he realized that it was just a typical list of provisions this time. Breathing a sigh of relief, he turned around and headed downstairs, trying his best to put Cindy out of his mind. He was just about to open the door to leave when he heard what sounded like a loud, muffled feminine scream coming from above him. Zayan stood there with his hand on the doorknob. Now was the turning point. He was a murderer, if he walked out now; he still had a chance to end this. He closed his eyes and quickly tried to weigh all the pros and cons. Finally deciding that self-preservation and his reputation were most important, Zayan opened the door and left.

Zeus watched the young woman walk up the stairs. She was frail, and the mold could detect a sickness in her. He did not care. He waited until his father had closed the door, and then he struck. Two tentacles of mold and filth rocketed out of the dark. One wrapped around the woman's lower part of her head, covering her mouth, while the other wrapped around her legs. She was jerked forward with such violence that the whiplash caused her to pass out. Zeus had the tentacles place the woman on his bed. Before he even realized what was happening, he was undressing her. Cindy woke up and tried to scream just as Zeus and a tentacle of mold started to sexually assault her.

Cindy was tortured for three days. Zeus even had the opportunity to get his hands bloody as well. He couldn't hold a knife, but the two digits on either hand did come to horrific sharp points. He did use his deformity to gouge out one of the woman's eyes. The most horrendous thing about the entire ordeal was how much Zeus enjoyed it. He had been locked away from the world his whole life. He had been told that he was not accepted in it. It felt beautiful to inflict pain and fear on someone that is not on his level of superiority. Yes, he would never look normal, but he had powers that only others could dream about. With those powers, he made millions of friends who had started to grow and prosper all over the apartment. The fungus and mold made quick work of Patricia's decaying body just as he knew his friends would take care of Cindy's corpse. That was the exact moment when Zeus stopped being a sociopath, and he became a full-fledged psychopath.

Zeus was oddly at peace following Cindy's death, having no desire to seek out more death and destruction. Rather, he requested a new television and a game console. He spent his days playing video games and talking with his friends, who pretty much overran the once pristine apartments. Zeus even started to leave the windows open when it rained, allowing the floorboards and walls to be soaked, creating the perfect scenario for mold and fungal colonies to grow. He never felt alone.

Three years later, during the spring of 2007, Zeus felt the overwhelming desire to kill again. And just as he did the first time, he requested a whore from Zayan. Zayan had found picking up a whore a little easier the second time, unlike last time. He had stopped earlier in the day with the bags of provisions before returning with the hooker. This woman appeared older. She was strung out when she climbed into the car. Zayan never bothered to get her name this time. When she began to walk upstairs, Zayan closed the door behind her. He went back to his home and quickly put the entire ordeal out of his mind.

Zeus kept this woman alive for almost two weeks, torturing her and using her for carnal and bloodletting pleasure. After her death, he felt the exact moment of peace from his other killing. Suicides at the bar had also stopped, eliminating the reputation of the trainyard being haunted.

Due to the horrible scent, Zayan had stopped going to the top of the stairs. The smell of mold and mildew was damn near choking. He knew that if Zeus would somehow die, the repairs to the place would be costly. For now, he was at his adult son's mercy. The third whore arrived in 2011, and Zayan delivered the woman with no trouble. It was during this time that Zeus made a very unusual discovery. The woman barely had time to react when Zayan closed the door behind her. Before she knew it, she had long tendrils of mold wrapped around her body, and she was being pulled upstairs.

Zeus subjected the young woman to various forms of torture for two days straight before he decided to try and see just how well he could control the woman. Using spores, he attempted to look from behind her eyes. That was when Zeus felt the pain she was feeling. The pain was intense. It caused him to detach his consciousness from the spores he had infected her body with. He had never felt what someone else was feeling. Sure, he had seen the world through other people's eyes, but he never felt what they were feeling. Confused at the new sensation, he once again entered the woman's body by way of spores. He discovered he could also feel physical pain as he felt the pain in her arm. Zeus remembered that he had broken her arm earlier. He smiled when the white bone ripped through her arm, causing a tiny rivulet of blood to flow. The pain from that wound was still severe, and he liked it. He tried to move the woman's arm. It caused her to shudder, and he realized just how much control he had.

Not only could Zeus choose a person's hallucination or influence their thoughts, but he also had a bit of control over them by way of some weird form of fungal possession. This new finding opened up an entire world of possibilities, but it would take some practice and some experimentation. Zeus did not mind; it simply meant he would have to keep his new plaything alive for just a little bit longer.

The woman, who was once a whore, and was now nothing but an emaciated shell of a human being, was manipulated via telepathic fungal spores. It took weeks, but Zeus could finally control the woman's body well enough to walk her down the stairs and out into the street totally under his control. He wondered how long he could stay inside another person this way as he led her down the street, not on the sidewalk but in the middle of the road. Zeus was still a bit clumsy in his navigation, but she was moving just fine. As she meandered through town, he heard the loud sound of a train whistle. While still in control of the woman's body, Zeus turned the head of his human puppet. When he smiled in his body, she smiled, so she did. She, as in he, sprinted towards the tracks. When the train was almost at the crossing, they leaped into the path of the oncoming train. Zeus had sent several people to their death this way through basic manipulation. Actually, throwing "himself" in front of the train was exhilarating. The pain was intense for just a brief second as the woman's body exploded. Immediately after, he found himself back in his own body.

"Oh my God!" he shouted into the empty room. "Did you see that?"

"Yes! "came the chorus of voices.

Zeus instantly felt extremely tired. He was the most exhausted he had ever been and decided that he did need to sleep. He figured doing what he had just done expended a lot of energy. Zeus was not truly aware of how much energy it had taken until he woke up almost two days later, but a full day nap was worth it. Now, he thought, the sadistic possibilities before him were endless. Fortunately for Zayan, Zeus never asked for a prostitute again.

Zayan was relieved that he was no longer receiving lists asking him for prostitutes. He was aware of the strange occurrences involving people who frequented the bar. He had a sneaky suspicion Zeus was behind them.

In 2014, a regular named Cathrine went to the bar. She appeared fine and in uplifting spirits. When she went home, her actions there caught everyone by surprise. She drowned both of her kids in the bathtub before taking her life by hanging herself.

In 2016, a young man celebrated his twenty-first birthday by attending his first-ever bar. After the celebration, he went home and shot both his parents to death before turning the gun on himself.

Also, in 2016, a young couple went into this bar. They stayed for five minutes with no signs of distress and promptly walked out. They walked directly behind the bar and stabbed each other to death. It was the most bizarre murder scene ever witnessed.

The owner of the bar was starting to feel troubled. No one blamed the bar for anything that happened. The bar owner felt maybe it was the atmosphere. There were a multitude of leaks that were beginning to spring up. He began pressuring Zayan to fix them. Zayan was unaware that Zeus opened the windows when it rained. All of the rain led to most of the damage. It allowed the floors upstairs to be coated in so much filth and mold that the wood floorboards had started to rot in areas causing leeks to spill in as it rained. Zeus, however, had become accustomed to the filth and dampness.

Zeus knew of the complaints and began to plug the leaks to avoid being found out. Zeus was infuriated when the owner decided it was time to sell the bar rights or even quit the bar scene altogether. The bar was a massive draw for Zeus. This drink-and-go atmosphere brought in countless people. There were always potential victims for him to use when he needed. One night in late 2019, the bar owner had closed the bar and counted his cash. Zeus (by way of fungal spores) convinced the man to continually consume large amounts of liquor. The bar owner finally collapsed behind the bar and died due to alcohol poisoning. Zeus was unsure if there was a backup plan to the bar opening up, but the owners' sons took over the bar a few weeks later, and people just came right back in.

Zayan continued to deliver goods to Zeus, but he no longer had to go beyond the bottom of the stairs. In 2020, something happened that affected everyone's lives.

The pandemic played havoc on everyone's lives. Zeus could follow the news from his computer that he kept in the front room, the only actual dry area in the apartment, but he grew confused. Diseases did not scare him, but they frightened everyone else. For two entire months, the bar lay empty. Zeus had become so bored without the people that he began to communicate with Zayan. Zayan, however, would not have a long conversation with Zeus. Zayan made an exception one day. He decided to discuss with Zeus that his mother had contracted Covid-19. Zeus was quite dismissive of the conversation; he did not care. The only concern Zeus had was to feed his desire for murder. Zeus was annoyed and overwhelmed with bloodlust that he almost killed Zayan.

Two weeks later, the bar finally reopened. That day Zayan also visited Zeus. He was coming with what he considered very devastating news. His wife and mother of Zeus had died due to Covid complications. Zeus paid no mind to this. He had his own victims to start focusing on.

That was the pattern of that building in Plano, IL, over the next two years. Zeus and Zayan's relationship of sundries and Zeus' manipulation of the lives of the bar patrons.

Zayan eventually evicted the sons who had taken over the bar. Zeus was, once again, furious until the day he noticed a young woman showed up and decided to reopen the bar under a different name. The day she opened her bar was a happy one for Zeus. It meant his sinister deeds could still carry on. His plan was thwarted when a pain in his chest struck him, resulting in him passing out.

When Zeus woke up, he found himself gasping for air. He realized that he was severely dehydrated. Zeus did not understand what had actually happened. He slowly made his way to his computer. Carefully, he climbed onto his chair and began to research. That was when he started to cough. Zeus moved his hand away from his mouth and noticed it was covered with a blackish-red mucus-like substance. Zeus continued to search as many websites as he could late into the night. He finally came to a diagnosis that disturbed him. While not too harmful in small amounts, mold and fungus could be toxic in large quantities. His home was covered. For the first time in a long time, he was afraid. He enjoyed his twisted, sinister way of life and did not want it to end. He was not ready to die. According to the internet, he had exposed himself to so many toxins his body was starting to break down. He did not know how much time he had left, but he wanted to figure out a way to live longer.

Zeus figured that there had to be a cure. After numerous hours of research, he discovered what spiritualists referred to as "Walk-ins." This is the act of taking over another person's body with your own spirit. This sounded like what he had technically been perfecting the past couple of years. Zeus wondered if the process could be permanent. As he continued his research, he found evidence that supported this theory; you could easily inhabit the body of another person long-term. This excited Zeus as he believed he had just discovered immortality. While not spiritual, he was definitely a being with psychic potential. He had already been transferring bits of his consciousness in mold and mushrooms. He recently discovered that taking over people using mold was just as easy. With the right amount of push, he could easily take over a person's body through a psychic walk-in. Maybe he wouldn't be in complete control, perhaps he would be, but at least he wouldn't be dead.

First, he needed to find the perfect host. The new owner of the bar, called April, was an ideal candidate. She was headstrong and had a steady determination one could admire and respect. With a new batch of regulars showing up, Zeus needed to study them all. This group of people was different from the others before them. Zeus discovered that several of these people were sturdy. Albeit not perfect specimens, some of these people smoked, which shortened lifespans, and some were extensive drinkers. Zeus was ready to just choose April until the night Cris arrived. Cris was sturdy and had no excessively unhealthy bad habits. Except, maybe for one. Cris loved his wife. Zeus could eliminate that problem if he wanted to, but not one he could currently see as feasible or beneficial. Zeus was going to have to watch these people for a while. He needed to truly study them. In the process, something happened that changed everything.

Zayan died.

Zeus went into a complete panic. His sole provider was gone. Although he could sneak food from the bar, things would be turned off without Zayan's money for the basics and utilities. He had about months of leeway before someone else would probably buy the building. Rumors were that April had her eye on it. If she bought it, that would mean she would come upstairs. That is when Zeus determined April is the obvious choice. He hesitated as he questioned whether she was strong enough. There had to be a way to test his theory. He mulled it over and was able to develop a plan.

Fortunately for Zeus, during the springtime, storms were frequent in Plano, Illinois. He knew he would have to find the strongest person to host his soul. He was dying, but he was determined to live on. He just had to be patient.

As predicted, the utilities were cut off. However, luck was currently on Zeus' side as no one had yet to come upstairs. Zeus went to work on his plan. Using the mold, he removed floorboards and weakened the overall structure of the building. He knew a storm would come. Zeus was well aware that he could use the storm shower to mask his sinister deeds as he committed one last heinous act in this bar. He continued to plan for this massacre.

The storm striking on the day of the bar's grand opening under the new name was just an unfortunate accident, but Zeus was beyond prepared. He had practiced what he was going to do numerous times. The electrocution of the one man was not planned, but it allowed Zeus time to coil tentacles around the three support beams just over the entrances. When the building began to shake, he instructed his allies to destroy those beams, sending debris crashing into the bar below. He was excited when he killed two people with the falling pieces. Zeus had to move quickly as there was no time to waste. Sending spores into the bar below, he influenced people to hallucinate or become quick to anger. Before he knew it, a massacre was unfolding before his eyes. The girls in the basement were out of reach of his spores, but a few tentacles would handle that problem for him. These people were doing what he truly hoped for. They gave in to their rage and their insecurities. They were so easily manipulated Zeus found it hilarious. The blood stained nearly every inch of the bar. As he watched, he grew an erection that sustained itself the entire time. The two men coming into the apartment were a nuisance, but that seemed to work itself out. And, now, here Zeus was, watching and enjoying the chaos he created. The violent evening had whittled itself down to four people. Zeus smiled; he had no doubt that his two top contenders would prevail to be his new host or body or whatever he was going to call it. Then it would be just a matter of time until there was only one left standing.

Then he would reveal himself.

Chapter 21: 2022 - The Final Fight

April flew across the pool table at a blinding speed, knife out in front of her, ready to drive it through Cris' chest. Cris immediately saw her coming and stepped backward with ease. April slid off the pool table, crashing to the floor, yet she felt nothing. She was back on her feet in a flash, holding the knife in front of her, ready to attack. Raising the ax ever so slightly, the handle blocked his chest, "You really want to do this bitch?" Cris saw the rage in April's eyes. A smile played across his lips.

"Fuck you, asshole," April hissed in a low menacing tone. "My kids are gone because of you. My friends. My bar. You are so going to die."

Zach raised the gun while slightly shaking. He glanced over at the bodies of George and Paul, suddenly overcome with a deep feeling of guilt. They were his friends; now, they lay dead by his hand. He looked at Mikey's body, trying to justify what he had done. Was it really all just a "heat of the moment" reaction? Tears welled up in his eyes as he turned towards Cris and April. He watched two people he had once called friends poised to fight each other to the death. Then Zach lost it.

"What the fuck is going on?" Zach shouted, still holding the gun upright. "Are we so fucking idiotic and pathetic that this is what we have come to? We can't be trapped in a bar for less than two hours before killing each other?" He shook his head, lowering it slightly. "Look around you. Friends and family, people we loved are fucking dead. And why? FUCKING WHY?"

Zach slowly moved around the edge of the pool table, unsurprised that neither Cris nor April did not respond, so he continued. "April, this is not like you. I get it; you're hurting. But come on." He looked over at Cris. "And, Cris, I get it. You're scared for your wife, but for fuck sake, the woman is kicking cancer's ass. A little temporary blindness is no reason to commit mass murder."

Cris lowered the ax contemplating what Zach had just said. Cris looked over his shoulder at his wife, now facing him. She blinked her eyes quickly before frantically saying, "Oh my God, Cris, I think my vision is coming back. Oh my God, Cris, I think...." Her eyes went wide, and she screamed, "Oh my God, Cris, LOOK OUT!"

Cris spun around with just enough time to dodge April as she lunged at him.

April had heard every word that Zach said. She lost her two children tonight. And no thanks to the actions of that asshole standing in front of her. Because of that, she did not care what Zach had to say. Her stomach was in knots over how she had brutally killed Jason. However, rage was all that was in her heart right now. April could probably spare Laura; Zach was safe, although he was getting on her nerves, he didn't do anything wrong. He did not deserve death by her hands. Deep in April's heart, she knew Zach was right, but she could not shake the feeling that Cris had to fucking die. Laura telling Cris her sight was returning distracted him enough to let his guard down. If ever there was a better time to strike, it was now. With the blade held outwards, both hands firmly gripping the handle, April charged towards Cris's exposed chest.

As another fight was about to rage upstairs in the bar, the fire was still blazing downstairs. Due to their age and dryness, the wood panels that lined the basement were reduced to embers. Flames were racing up the walls and spreading across the basement ceiling. The stairs that April fought so hard to climb up earlier were now wholly engulfed in flames. Portions of the stairs had started to collapse. The charred remains of those who had fallen into the basement or were killed there were also now burning, adding kindling to the fire. Flames had even started to eat their way through the floor of the main bar area, especially behind the service bar. No one noticed the fire because after April tried to drive her knife through Cris's heart, they were all focused on each other.

Cris stepped aside as the knife slid across his forearm, leaving a deep two-inch gash. Blood trickled from the wound. He hissed through his teeth as he turned and stepped back while April skidded to a halt. She turned to ready the knife for another attack. Laura decided that was her moment. She ran over and grabbed April by the hair with both hands. Laura attempted to drag the woman to the floor.

Zach raised the gun while trying to make his way over to the two women. "Let her go, Laura!" he commanded.

Cris stepped in front of Zach, warning, "Stop pointing that gun at my wife."

Zach looked at Cris shaking his head. "This is how it has to end? Really?" Zach raised the gun and looked down at the ground, taking Cris's eyes off. That proved to be a costly mistake. Cris, holding the ax in his left hand when Zach lowered his eyes, his instincts kicked in. Cris quickly snatched up the bloody cue ball (that had managed to stay on the pool table during the entire melee) with his right hand and, the precision aim he was known for, threw the cue ball as hard as he could at Zach's face.

Zach looked up just in time for the cue ball to strike him in the nose. His nose practically exploded while his right orbital bone shattered. Blood flowed from his ruined nose, and he reacted how anyone else would have. He dropped the gun, letting it fall under the pool table while bringing his hands to his now shattered nose. Cris quickly cleared the three steps he was from Zach. Before Zach's vision could restore itself from the tears in his eyes, Cris had gripped the ax in both hands and brought it down in the center of Zach's skull. The force was so great that Zach's left eyeball popped out from the already weakened socket caused by the cue ball's impact. Cris held the ax in Zach's head, watching the blood flow from the wound for a moment before violently ripping the ax free. Zach's body hit the ground just as Laura started screaming.

April struggled against Laura's grip and pushed back against her. The two women began falling backward into the dart area. April collapsed on top of Laura, and Laura let out a loud "ooof" as all the air was driven from her body. She let go of April's hair, allowing April to roll off of Laura. April got to her knees, turned, and viciously slammed the butcher knife down into the center of Laura's chest. Laura started to scream a bloodcurdling squeal. April pulled the blade free and slammed her weapon down again into the center of Laura's throat, effectively silencing the woman.

Upon hearing his wife scream, Cris turned around just in time to see April plunge the knife into Laura's throat. "NO!" He shouted, and he raced over towards his wife. April pulled the knife free, rolling out of the way. Cris fell to his knees and cradled his wife's head. "No, no, no!" he cried out repeatedly. April quickly returned her feet and walked back into the main bar area. She noticed a small column of smoke rising from behind the service bar. That was when she remembered the basement was on fire. April needed to end this madness and fast. She was aware that Cris would probably overpower her. April determined that if she was going to stand a chance, she needed Kevin's gun. She scanned the room and saw Zach's body on the ground, blood pooling on the floor around the gaping wound in his head, but she did not spot the gun. Figuring it had fallen under the pool table, she began to kneel down when Cris, without any warning, erupted in a loud primal scream behind her.

Cris held Laura's head, but he knew it was too late. She looked up at him, and he could see the panic in her eyes. Blood bubbled from between her lips, running like rivers from the corner of her mouth. She gasped twice then she was gone. Cris lowered her head gently to the ground, leaned over, and kissed her forehead. He stood up, snatched up the ax, and screamed with hate and determination.

April turned when Cris began marching in her direction. He moved with a quickness she had never seen. Cris was virtually on top of her in seconds, raising the ax high above his head. "You fucking bitch," he bellowed. "I am going to fucking enjoy killing you."

April rolled out of the way as he brought the ax down, where it sank harmlessly into the top of the bar. The ax sunk a good two inches deep into the bar's wood. Cris tried to yank it free, but it did not come loose. That was when April attacked.

The way Cris was standing gave April a perfect target to strike. She sunk the blade into his back with ease. Cris let out a yelp of pain. He let go of the ax momentarily and pushed her off of him. April never let go of the knife. As Cris pushed her off, she took the butcher knife with her. His flesh tore him open, blood instantly began to soak the back of his shirt, warm blood spurting from the wound in his back.

Cris turned and faced her, "You fucking stabbed me." He turned to try and free the ax once more. April wasted no time and again lunged towards Cris. She aimed the blade a little higher. This time the knife stabbed deeply into the right side of Cris's neck. Cris stopped trying to free the ax from the bar and pushed April off of him again. April lost her grip on the knife and fell towards the floor, where she landed quite roughly on her rear end.

Blood poured from the wound in Cris's neck as he stared down at April. He raised his right hand up and pulled the knife free from his neck without thinking. Blood erupted from the wound like a geyser. He seemed unfazed as he walked towards April, his hand grasping the knife handle tightly. Blood was steadily flowing from the gaping wound he left behind when he freed the blade. He could feel the warmth of the blood as it washed over him. He was capable of flashing April a sinister smile, "Fine, ok," he said as blood flowed from the corner of his mouth. "You killed me, but I got you bitch." He raised the knife high into the air, ready to bring it down on April as she was trying to scramble back to her feet. April raised her hands, readying herself for the blow she knew would come.

Suddenly the ceiling above the bar and kitchen section collapsed and it was at that exact moment that the real absolute horror came out to play.

Chapter 22: 2022 - Three In A Bed

Debris rained down, destroying several bottles of alcohol, one television, half of the kitchen appliances, and some sports memorabilia April kept on the wall. Cris stopped shifting his body, looked over his shoulder, and watched as four black tentacle-looking appendages pulsated out from the new hole in the ceiling. They slowly flowed towards the ground. A four-foot-tall nude man emerged from the gaping void in the ceiling, feet first. He appeared to be floating. The tentacles that seemed to be growing from his back controlled his entire descent. Once the man had made his full emergence while hovering in the air, Cris and April realized he was using the tentacles as a set of extra arms and legs.

Dizzy from the blood loss, disoriented, and now completely confused, Cris dropped the knife, falling to his knees. Not once did Cris take his eyes off the little man that just appeared out of the ceiling.

Meanwhile, April, still sitting on the floor, stared at the man, her jaw agape, eyes wide, tried to speak. All she could muster was, "What the fuck?"

The man spoke to them in a condescending tone, "Hi April. Hi Cris. My name is Zeus. My home or prison rather is right above you. I was my father's dirty little secret. I never once thought I could ever be part of this world. But now, thanks to one of you, I am ready to find my place in society."

April had not taken her eyes off of him. In fact, she may not have yet even blinked. One thing for sure was that she did not understand what was going on. The man-like creature that called himself Zeus clapped his hands together. April noticed his hands resembled lobster claws before he spoke once more. "Well, let's get this over with. Like most good things, this night has to come to an end."

Cris's eyes were rolling into the back of his head as he tried to stay awake. He heard the little man who descended from the ceiling talking. Cris could tell he was losing the battle with death and would bleed out at any moment.

"Aww, man," Cris heard the man-like creature thing say. "I really hoped he would have won."

Cris collapsed forward. As he stared at April, he felt all the rage leave his body. Cris did not know why he had been so mad. He was perplexed. He did know that he was going to die and that soon he would be with his wife once more. Cris opened his mouth and weakly said, "April. I'm sorry," before dying in a pool of his blood.

Zeus looked at April, "No matter. You will do just fine."

April continued to stare at the tiny freak of a man suspended in the air by what looked to be the same black tentacles that attacked her in the basement. He looked like he was swaying in the air. The tentacles were shifting his weight. Meanwhile, another sizable black tentacle crawled over the service bar, slithering towards April. Several images ran together through April's mind. The only cohesive thought she could utter was, "What do you mean I'll do?"

The man chuckled and, with a laugh, "You're the perfect specimen for me to take over. You see, I may not look like much, but I can promise you my mind is a world beyond anything you have ever experienced." While he spoke, the tentacle inched closer to April. She slowly backed up, still trying to get to her feet, pushing herself backward while seated on the floor. She grimaced as he called her a specimen. If he kept talking, she thought, maybe she could find a way out of this. She stayed silent as he continued. "You see, dear, I am dying; well not me, my body. I could live on in mold and maybe something else. But I found out that I can actually possess human beings. All I have to do is take over the ideal body, and I am free. Cris was my first choice, but don't feel bad. You always were a close second. Good thing I orchestrated this fight to the finish. I almost wound up in a weaker body."

Realization washed over April. Somehow this little thing had caused all of this. He was responsible for everything. April nervously looked around on the floor, searching for Kevin's gun. She believed, at this point, it was her only hope. April noticed that the tentacle moved slower the more the little thing that called himself Zeus talked. She thought to herself that he really seemed to enjoy hearing himself speak. If she could just keep him talking, it would distract him. "So, you're saying you caused this?" April timidly asked.

"That's what I said. That black mist you guys breathed in before you could get your masks on, which you all forgot about, by the way, was actually spores from my friends." Zeus looked over and lovingly caressed one of the tentacles on his left. "All this time, I was afraid to be among you because of what I saw you doing to each other when at any moment I could have just bent your little sheepish minds to my will. I mean, you guys are so easy to divide. I gave you guys a little panic, a little fear. Some suggestive voices, an imaginary llama, then I amped your rage by just ten percent, and you idiots fucking killed each other. I am shocked that it was really that easy."

April felt warmth spreading underneath her, and suddenly she remembered the basement was engulfed in flames. She stared over at the basement door, getting a very unpleasant thought. She knew that she had no way of getting out of her alive now. If it was possible to break the hold fear had on her, she could jump to her feet and run to the basement door and plummet headfirst. If she died, then the little shit that caused all of this carnage on her grand opening celebration would have no human to take and would also die. With one arm, she reached up and grabbed the edge of the pool table, pulling herself upright. Her legs were shaking, but she had one more fight to finish.

Zeus noticed her standing and smiled. "Oh ho, look at you. I knew you were ok. For a moment, I thought you were broken."

"Fuck you," April hissed.

"Yeah, I know, I know. You're angry, and you should be." Zeus continued, "But not really at me. I mean, yeah, yeah. I led people you love to their death. But, you see, my father left me upstairs. He paid some bitch to pretend to care about me. I was the one left behind. Hey, at least your children died knowing their mother loved them. I didn't even know who my mother was. Do you know what it feels like to know you were nothing but a dirty secret to your parents?" Zeus shook his head, trying to avoid tears swelling up in his eyes. April noticed the tentacle had stopped moving. She had to keep him talking; she had to keep him distracted.

"What?" April gasped, doing her best to mimic sounding empathetic. "You're dad did this? That's horrible. I would never!"

"Who knows?" Zeus waved his disfigured hands in the air. "Maybe he was right to hide me. Because honestly, you people are just terrible to each other. I never stood a chance. But if he showed me just an ounce of love, maybe, just maybe, I wouldn't have done this." He took a deep breath and smiled," But," he said with a cheery voice," I might not have discovered what I can do. I mean, I control mold and fungus and human minds. Your comment proves that you two were on the same wavelength and had the potential to be better than what I experienced, which is odd. But hey, whatever. The past is the past, and this is now. Also, let's be honest. There are no guarantees that I wouldn't have discovered a need to watch things die." He paused and looked over, noticing April was not in the same spot. "Oh my hell, where do you think you're going?"

April took advantage of Zeus's distracted monologue and decided it was now or never. She turned and ran towards the basement door. April heard Zeus call out to her but figured there was enough of a head start to get to the door in time. As she grabbed the doorknob, she heard a hissing sound while her palm burned. The flames must have crept up to the door. That brief hesitation cost her dearly as a tentacle abruptly appeared over her shoulder, slamming into the door.

Zeus sensed what April was planning and called out to her, "Suicide? Really?"

April ducked under the tentacle, running back towards the pool table when the oddest thought occurred, and she started laughing.

"What's so funny?" Zeus petitioned.

"Even if you take me over," April started," You are still fucking stuck in here with me. How in the hell do you hope to get out?"

Zeus chuckled that sinister-sounding chuckle once more, replying, "I'll crawl out one of the windows."

April stopped laughing and turned around. For the first time all night, she glanced over at the large window next to the main entrance. She had completely forgotten about it. They all had. It was just glass and wood, and all someone had to do was turn a latch. The window would have easily opened. Nothing had blocked the window. The opening was big enough that practically everyone could have crawled out to safety. Thinking about it, April was also now pretty confident that the second window by the other entrance near the dartboards was also unblocked and easily accessed. Tears welled up in April's eyes, "How could I have forgotten about that?" she thought.

"Because I wanted you too," she heard Zeus say, only it felt like he was much closer. Closer, as if he was practically in her head. April turned around and looked at Zeus, still swaying in the air behind the bar. The tentacles looked like they were rocking him back and forth. "I am already in your head, dear." April heard his voice once again, and as if to show her he was in her head, he reached up with the one long digit on his right hand tapped his temple. Zeus clapped his hands once more and spoke aloud, "See, blocking the door was easy. That would be my fault. I let so much rain in and all that filth upstairs that the rot just spread. I had to keep the windows available, so conveniently,

I just had you guys overlook them." Zeus let out a sinister laugh and then continued. "That's the thing about anger and fear. Once you are overwhelmed with either emotion, you overlook the easiest solution to your problem. Like I said earlier, you idiots made this too easy."

April shook her head and screamed. "NO!"

Zeus, still smiling, said, "Ok, well, that's your opinion, but I am pretty sure our time is limited because I hear sirens! Let's get this over with."

April paused and was relieved to hear them as well. She turned and prepared to make a beeline towards the window to throw herself through it when a tentacle of black mold coiled itself around her ankles and pulled her to the ground. Her chin connected sharply with the floor, and her vision darkened. She fought off unconsciousness and kept her eyes open as Zeus slowly dragged her towards him. In what appeared to be her final act of desperation, April grabbed the leg of the pool table she was near and held fast. April tried pulling herself away from him, but it felt she would lose the battle. Her heart quickened when she saw Kevin's gun. It had fallen and slid slightly under the pool table. April let go of the pool table leg and reached out for the weapon. She had never felt that strong sense of relief as she did when she wrapped her hands around the gun's handle. April was securing her grip just as she felt her legs start to slide up over Zach's corpse.

Suddenly, red and blue lights started to flash through the bar. April had only one chance to survive. She rolled over onto her back and pointed the gun directly at Zeus.

Zeus let out a little cackle, "Really, bitch? I cannot be defeated. I am better than...."

"Fuck you, freak!" April interrupted Zeus and pulled the trigger.

The gunshot was deafening. The recoil caught April off guard, causing her to drop the gun. Thank God her aim was true. The bullet struck Zeus smack in the center of his forehead, effectively silencing him. April watched as his head essentially exploded. Instead of a shower of blood and gore, a cloud of black mist erupted where his skull once was. The tentacle loosened around her leg. April tried to kick herself backward. As Zeus' body swayed over the bar and then collapsed towards her. April screamed, holding up her hands before what remained of Zeus landed on top of her. His body and the four tentacles that supported him exploded in a very dense cloud of what April now knew was black spores. She closed her eyes, held her breath, and pushed her legs against the floor harder, but the cloud still covered her.

April was covered in the black filth only for a moment before she could get on her feet. She was coughing, trying to hack up the bits that made it into her nostrils. The stuff had gotten into her eyes, and its coarseness stung. Tears began to wash down her cheeks. Her vision was blurry, but she realized spores covered her as April looked down at her arms. She began to brush herself off when she looked up and saw the window. Without thinking, she ran towards the window, throwing herself into it.

This window, made out of an aging wood frame and simple glass, shattered under her weight as she jumped through it. April found herself tumbling to the sidewalk below. The glass sliced her skin, causing several open wounds on her arms and head. She hit the sidewalk with a thud. April tried to get to her feet but couldn't because she was too weak. She attempted to look around, but in her blurred vision, all she saw was the bright blue and red lights from the three first responder vehicles that had just arrived.

She heard a familiar voice call out to her. "April, is that you?"

April couldn't quite place the voice, and she didn't care right now. She blindly reached out in the direction of the voice, pleading, "Get it off of me," before finally passing out.

Chapter 23: 2022 - Help Arrives

Brandon had been a paramedic at the Little Rock-Fox FPD, Station One, for three years, and he loved his job. The station was located two streets up from The 4/26, a bar that he enjoyed visiting on his days off. As often as he frequented the bar, he had developed a friendship with quite a few patrons. Tonight though was not a night to worry about drinks. A storm had just ravaged the small town of Plano, which kept very busy. All available units were needed because there might be a possibility of a mass casualty event. Brandon didn't even think about the bar or its people while he was working. Two hours later, when his ambulance headed back to the station from dropping off a young woman who was lucky to survive a car accident, his truck received a call that the roof of The 4/26 had collapsed and that there were reports of gunfire.

Brandon quickly sat upright in the passenger seat as his partner Ryan clicked on the overhead lights and siren and raced down Route 34. Thankfully the streets were empty. They found themselves turning down Hale street in a matter of moments. On their next turn, they flew down Main street. The moment Brandon saw what had happened to his beloved 4/26, his heart dropped.

The roof had caved in. Brandon could see that the second floor would completely collapse down into the first at any second. While no one was on the street, he recognized all the cars still there. It appeared that no one had left, and everyone was trapped inside. Columns of smoke rose in the air, making the matter even more urgent. Brandon was well aware that where there is smoke, there is fire. Brandon's ambulance came to a halt when a ladder truck from his home station pulled around the corner, followed closely behind by a police car.

Brandon jumped out of the ambulance and looked up at the building, realizing that they did not have long to get everyone out. His thoughts were interrupted by a gunshot that rang out from inside the bar. The first responders flinched and ducked. One of them shouted, "What the fuck was that?" as glass shattered, followed by the thud of someone slamming into the concrete sidewalk. Brandon raced around what he knew to be Kevin's green van. That was when he saw Apri on the sidewalk screaming something.

"April! Is that you?" Brandon shouted. He raced over to her. As he approached April, he noticed about a dozen wounds all over her body. She was bleeding a lot, but not enough to where it would become a fatal amount of blood loss.

Brandon stared intensely as April looked up at him. In a partially shouting voice, "Get it off of me!" she cried and then passed out. Brandon caught her head just before it hit the ground just as his partner joined him.

"What did she say?" Ryan asked.

"She said to get it off of me," Brandon answered confusedly.

"The glass? Because that's all over her." Ryan replied, trying to figure it out.

Brandon looked down at April and saw that Ryan was right. But the way she was brushing her skin and face made him think that maybe April was talking about something else. At that moment, a loud splintering noise began to sound out overhead.

"You boys need to move now," a loud voice commanded from behind them. Brandon looked up, seeing the top of the damaged building shift. Knowing he shouldn't, he felt that he had no choice at this point. Brandon scooped April up in his arms and ran into the street just as the second floor entirely collapsed into the first. Flames appeared, igniting pieces of the old dried wood. Within an instant, the entire bar was on fire. Firefighters were scrambling to douse the fire. While Brandon carried April back to the ambulance, he knew that The 4/26 was no more.

April opened her eyes. She saw that she was no longer in the bar, or outside the bar for that matter. She was in the center of a strange room; there was no furniture, and the walls were bare. The ceiling and floor were painted black. April could feel the ground beneath her feet as she walked. She understood that she was physically somewhere, even if it felt as if she was trapped in a void. "Hey, where am I?" she asked out loud.

Yet, no answer came.

"Anyone there?" she called. Again, nothing but silence. April walked over to the wall on her left. She discovered what covered the wall was not black paint. Instead, the walls were covered in whatever filth the tentacles that attacked her were made out of. She quickly pulled back with a look of disgust and fear, fighting back a scream. Suddenly a familiar voice spoke up behind her. "Hello, April," it said.

April turned around. She now stood in the center of the room. She could make out that the small man who claimed responsibility for the massacre at her bar was there, too. He moved and was now standing in the center of the room, staring straight at her.

"Wait, wait, you're dead!" April stuttered. "Where.... am....I?" She looked around, confused, trying to understand.

The man smiled, walked over to the wall where April was standing, and caressed the black filth almost lovingly. April noticed that his hands still resembled lobster claws. As the man looked up at her, he said, "We're in your head; you know what? I think I am going to like it here."

April started to scream, the most bloodcurdling scream one could bear.

April sat straight up, still screaming when she realized she was lying in a hospital bed. She scanned the room and recognized she was in a hospital. She laid her head back down, trying to catch her breath. "It was a dream. Just a dream," she thought to herself. Then she heard the door opening.

Brandon was standing outside the hospital room when he heard April scream. He quickly opened the door and saw she was breathing heavily, as she obviously had a nightmare.

"April," he said in a soft voice. "Are you okay?"

April slowly turned her head to look over at the voice she heard. She smiled when she saw Brandon. He walked over to her and put his hand on her shoulder. April tried to reach up to touch his hand, but she discovered she was handcuffed to the bedrail. "What the hell?" she questioned aloud.

Brandon frowned as he looked down at her, "April, you're the only one that made it out." He shook his head and continued with kind eyes and a soft voice. "It looked like a scene from a warzone. In fact, a horror movie may describe it better. The handcuffs are just a precaution, dear. But I am glad you're doing okay."

The door opened once more. Two police officers followed what seemed to be a detective in the room.

"Hello, April. I am Detective Johnson." The man she assumed was a detective spoke. "Look, when you feel up to it, I will need you to tell me what happened. Until then, we will have to keep you monitored and working on getting better," he explained as he gestured towards her cuffed arm.

Brandon smiled and looked at April before speaking. "I called your attorney. I'll stay here if you need me to."

April shook her head. With a very hoarse voice, she said, "It's okay. Just get me something to drink, and I'll talk."

The detective nodded to one of the officers in command to have him appease her request. He took a seat in a chair in the corner of the room. The officer quickly returned with a cup of ice water. April accepted the water, drinking greedily. Brandon reached out to hold

April's hand, and April squeezed his hand tightly. She took a deep breath and began to tell her story.

Epilogue: 2022-2023 - A Hard Year

Although she was sure to tell her side of the story, the following year was a rough one for April as she was still arrested for negligence and fifteen separate involuntary manslaughter charges. She made certain to explain to the officers about the freak that lived upstairs, but she left out the tentacles of mold; because that just sounded, well, crazy.

The bar was a complete loss. The firefighters fought gallantly to maintain and then put out the blaze. Sadly, the barroom floor was so weak from the flames that the first floor collapsed ten minutes into the firefight, sending everything plummeting into the basement. At that point, the brave responders worked diligently to keep the fire from spreading. At 9:15 the following morning, they managed to snuff out the last bit of the fire. Left behind was nothing more but a smoldering crater full of debris and corpses.

Clean-up and recovery efforts took nearly two weeks. April was released from the hospital and police custody when the last body was recovered. Identifying the bodies took a little bit longer, though. Within a month, every corpse was identified... except for four.

The police were baffled by the appearance of the four unknown corpses. As a matter of fact, they weren't so much corpses as they were dismembered skeletal remains of people who suffered something horrible. As the police tried to put the pieces of this puzzle together, they believed that April had given them a detailed account of everyone who had shown up. These four had to have come from somewhere.

Two months later, April was able to bury her children; she cried the entire time.

Brandon attended every funeral service for his fallen friends. Each night after the services, he went to a small bar in Sandwich to order a drink and cried.

The police continued to investigate and eventually determined that Zayan was responsible for the sad state of disrepair that the building was in. They ultimately shifted blame onto him, clearing April on all charges. The four unknown corpses were determined to have been in the apartments upstairs. This led the police to conclude why Zayan forbade anyone from venturing upstairs. Zayan was labeled a serial killer from these findings. The assets left behind in his estate, which had not been claimed, were seized by the state. Any remaining funds were used to cover the costs of the funerals and retribution for April's business losses.

In the coming months, anytime anyone saw April, they all said she looked different. She wasn't herself. She grew more and more distant from Joel, showing no signs of intimacy towards him. Joel figured it was just PTSD. He decided it was better not to push the issue; however, he caught her talking to herself a few times. But given the trauma she had recently endured, he just left it alone.

As the year anniversary of the tragedy approached, April essentially withdrew herself from the world. Joel let her be, but he had been looking into getting her counseling because it was time for her to start healing.

On the night of the anniversary of the massacre at The 4/26, Brandon led a candlelight vigil. They gathered at the now vacant lot of which the bar once stood. Although the city decided to turn the place into a garden, the plants had just been planted, so they were not yet in bloom. Once they did, it would be a moving tribute to the lives that were lost.

Joel and April did not attend the memorial. Instead, Joel was heading home from work. April sent him a two-word, provocative text message, "I'm Horny." Joel was excited; he had not been intimate with April for a year, and it seemed she was finally ready.

When Joel walked into the house, the lights were off, with only a few candles lit. The air smelled fresh but oddly musty. At this moment, he did not mind. Instead, he hurried to their bedroom, undressing as he went. He found April waiting for him, nude, sitting seductively on the edge of the bed. Using her pointer finger, she motioned Joel to come over to her. Without any hesitation, he did. When he approached her where she could reach him, April pulled him close to her, kissing him deeply. They fell back onto the bed. April released him from her grasp as Joel began to kiss her neck. Slowly she reached her right hand underneath her pillow and grabbed the handle of the butcher knife she had hidden there earlier.

April positioned herself on top of Joel. With a quick and precise stroke, April removed her hand from under the pillow and buried the blade into the side of Joel's neck. Joel pushed her off, spraying April with his blood. He covered his neck wound with his right hand, got his feet under him, and tried to back away. April acted quickly and was on top of him, driving him to the ground. Joel fell onto his back. April straddled him and proceeded to stab him in any place she could find. The knife sliced through Joel's chest, face, and arms. After it was all said and done, April stabbed Joel thirty-eight times, and she smiled the entire time.

When April had her fill with butchering him and knew that Joel was dead, she got off of him and stood over, admiring his bleeding, mutilated body. His blood soaked both her and the carpet. She began to laugh before saying out loud, "There; did I do good?"

A chorus of voices that only April could hear spoke back. "Yesss," they sang.

April turned, faced her bed, and smiled as a long black tentacle of mold slithered out from underneath.

THE END

Author's Notes: Fun Facts Are Fun

Author's notes, or what I like to call mindless dribble from manic thoughts, have become the norm in all my books. Usually, I write anthologies. At the end of each book, I write what inspired each individual story. But this book is different.

This book is a novel. I pretty much covered all the inspiration for this book in the introduction. But I feel that a little fact-checking would be in order. So let me reveal to you the truths about a lot of stuff in this book.

As I mentioned earlier, Pub 4-26 is real. It does have an American flag mural painted on its side. It does have abandoned apartments with rain damage above it. The dartboard layout is pretty close to how I described it; the arcade golf machines and the electronic slots are all there. Alas, there is no basement dance floor and no expanded kitchen. The basement houses the hot water heater and supplies; that's about it. Pub 4-26's kitchen is small and basic, but the food that comes from it is really good.

Main Street in Plano is almost exactly how I described it. I took a few liberties and left some businesses out. There is a pet store on Main Street. Batcave Treasures is an actual place you can visit. I hear they carry the books of a particular author you might like..... Me..... I'm the author. Gotta love shameless plugs.

The train tracks behind the bar exist. As far as I know, there is no urban legend surrounding the tracks in relation to suicides.

The names of the dart teams are also accurate except for one. Drew and Becka's team is not called Two Chix and a Dick. It is actually Two

Dix and a Chick. Their other teammate is male. Mikey was a sub for them, though.

Zayan, his wife, Zeus, Patricia, George, Paul, Keith, David, Blake, and Detective Johnson are fictional characters. They were made up for either plot devices or because I need more people.

Lori, Jason, Sarah, Candy, Paco, Barb and Michelle are based on real people, but the names were changed due to one reason or another (most of those reasons are not worth repeating). I have nothing else really to add to that subject, so let's move on.

April is real, very real, and many of the things I mention in this book are also real. She is the owner of the bar. As of the moment of writing this, she has a boyfriend named Joel. April is a friendly, caring person. But don't get it twisted; you cross her, and she will fuck you up. She doesn't like it when people take the lord's name in vain. Her birthday is April 26th, as well as one of her children's. Thus, the bar's name. Also, she will fight to the death to defend those she loves. She is a wonderful human being and just a good friend. And no, I am not kissing ass for a free beer.

Becka and Drew are a real couple (one of the two power couples at the bar, if I can be honest) and real people. Becka actually edited this book and added a lot of the subtle nuances about people I didn't pick up on. Becka is sweet-natured, and Drew is an all-around nice guy. The betting part, along with Drew losing nearly all of them, actually happened. They also host karaoke at Pub 4-26 every other Saturday night. They have supported my writing career immensely, whether by sharing a link to my books on social media or allowing their daughter to appear on one of my other books' covers. They have been true friends. Thanks, guys.

Laura and Cris are another of the bar's power couples. Laura was actually the first person I held a full-length conversation with. Everything about her kicking Cancer's ass is true. She is a strong woman everyone loves, and she does actually let out a loud "WOOT WOOT" when her team is doing well. Cris is also loud, just the way I describe. He was chosen as my villain simply because of his booming, competitive nature. I also know, as does everyone, he would kill to protect his wife. He's also the guy with the ax on the cover.

Christian and Lucy are another couple. Lucy does not go often, but Christian frequents the bar to support his mother, April. Lucy, I think, is the most excited about this book. Christian is the dead guy on the cover. I tried to do them justice; I think I did.

Stacie and Ernie are two people I am happy to call friends. Stacie is a horror geek, while Ernie has not met anything he can't fix. Great people. Just the absolute best.

Eric and Hope, are another actual couple and people I enjoy drinking with.

Dustin and Holly. Oh man, my beloved teammates. Dustin asked if I could have Holly kill him, so hey, wished granted bro.

Kevin is based on me. I am not suicidal. I just needed to get the gun in there. Please don't read too much into it.

Mikey, oh man, what is there to say about Mikey. She is a wonderful soul, and the backstory I gave her is happening. If I have a best friend, Mikey, is it.

Deanne and Mark. Yesss, Deanne was my son's bus driver. She was the one who invited me to the bar in the first place. Yes, she is a bartender there. Yes, she breaks her ankles. I love her to death. Mark is her husband, who is just a good dude. The blow pop is an inside joke that everyone in this story gets. We will leave it at that.

Zach is also an actual person, and everything about his electrical and HVAC experience is true. If Pub 4-26 had a Jiminy Cricket, it would be him.

Robbie is another bartender at the bar and is a breath of fresh air. He is funny and just a good guy to talk to. Also, he doesn't smoke. I just made that a cheap plot device.

Billy, Jeremy, Brett, A.J., and Sherri, are all real people and people who I am happy to call friends. I have shared many laughs and drinks with them.

Nikole, Jennifer, and Tanya are real as well. They are all bartenders for the bar. Nikole is April's daughter, while Jennifer is her niece. Tanya still complains about the bloodstain the cover shoot left behind.

Kory, Kyle, and Danny (whose name is changed for personal reasons) are all regulars, and they practically rent a far corner of the bar.

Randy is mentioned in the Welcome to The 4/26 chapter. He is the gentleman that is in charge of many dart leagues in the surrounding area of Plano, IL.

Now, there are a few characters who appeared in the Zeus chapters that are real:

Tony is the daytime bartender, and he is a good guy, a great guy.

Mike is the actual current mayor of Plano and even helped direct traffic for the cover shoot.

Jamal is an Alderman and a dear friend of mine and a 4-26 patron. He supports all the businesses in Plano, so he is everyone's regular.

Austin, I met after I started this project and just grew to like the guy. I wish I had a more prominent part for him, but hey, he gets a mention.

The paramedic Ryan is based on a dear friend of mine who is an actual paramedic and is overseas in Poland aiding Ukraine refugees. I pray for his safety and choose to honor him here.

Brandon, well, if you read the dedication, then you know about Brandon.

Well, that's it. Thank you guys so much for reading. I hope you like it. I have nothing more to say. This book started on September 15th, 2021 and was finally finished on March 18th, 2022, my first novel. I am just ecstatic at its completion. Hug those you love tightly, and be nice to the mold underneath your bed. Until next time.

Toodles,

Kevin

About the Author

Kevin Densmore is an Author in a small town in Illinois. A customer at the real Pub 4/26 and a below average dart player. This is his thirteenth published work and is his first novel.

Read more at https://books2read.com/rl/WYaLOW.

Lightning Source UK Ltd.
Milton Keynes UK
UKHW010626270422
402137UK00001B/179

9 798201 162108